MURDER
WITH A
TWIST

A BLAKE SISTERS TRAVEL MYSTERY – BOOK 3

CARTER FIELDING

Published by Carter Fielding Press
5237 River Road, #304
Bethesda, MD 20216

Editing, design, and production by Bublish, Inc.
ISBN: eBook -978-1-647045-67-8
Paperback- 978-1-647045-95-1

For information about the author and her projects
please visit:
www.mcarterfielding.com

"Lend yourself to others but
give yourself to yourself."

Montaigne

POWDERY, GOLDEN DUST FROM THE nearby parched fields mixed with sweat and streaked her face with muddy rivulets. Finley Blake knew she was making the matter worse by running the back of her hand over her face, but it kept the sweat beads out of her eyes so she could get a clear shot. She imagined what her mother would say if she saw her. Something about ladies never sweating, only glistening. Bull hockey. This was sweat, plain and simple.

"Can you catch them in this light? I fear the subtle color might wash out." Dr. Sanat Rao pointed to the dark-gray patches of paint that animated the white stucco face of the house with stylized beasts amid intricate swirls and patterns. He was a slight, Indian man in his early thirties with delicate features and a balding pate.

"I think we have just enough sun to catch the contrast." Finley adjusted the aperture on her camera just in case the light faded in the last few minutes.

She had been working with Dr. Rao for the past three months, trying to understand and record the historical and artistic significance of the wall paintings of the Adivasi tribe. What had started as a short spread for a travel magazine had grown into a multiregional series as Finley started to understand the artistic ties that linked India together, especially in Bihar, Jharkhand, and Odisha.

The paintings she was focusing on for this segment of the series were mud art forms that were most prevalent in Jharkhand, especially around Hazaribagh and Jamshedpur. Uncovered for modern audiences in the early 1990s by cultural activist, Bulu Imam, they had been part of the decorative arts in India for centuries. With tribal populations dispersing and their art forms practiced less, there was concern that the *Khovar* designs, which were related to weddings, and *Sohrai* art forms, more associated with the harvest, would be lost.

"That should do it for today." Finley removed the filters and placed them in her case as she spoke. "We can get the other *Sohrai* paintings tomorrow. They favor brighter light."

"I cannot begin to thank you for your interest in preserving these tribal mural styles. They are becoming a dying art."

Finley pulled a handkerchief out of her bag and wiped her face, applying considerable pressure to roll off the layers of dirt that had become encrusted on her skin.

"As long as daughters get married, I suspect mothers will be painting on the walls. The tradition has survived this many millennia." She closed up her camera bag and rose from her crouched position. "It will take a while for it to die out completely."

"I hope," Dr. Rao said softly.

Despite his youth, he was a leading scholar in the field and had been studying tribal murals for several years. Part of his willingness to be Finley's advisor and guide for this effort was his desire to raise to the Indian and global community the need for structured preservation programs across the country as tribal populations decreased.

"When must you return to Delhi?" Dr. Rao looked up from packing away the rest of the equipment.

He realized he enjoyed having a companion in the field with him. Someone who understood the esoteric intricacies of his area of study. Someone who didn't laugh at him when his voice grew treble and his face reddened as he talked with great stridency about the loss to humanity if tribal women stopped painting and their men stopped drumming.

"Not for another week or so. We have to finish here and then head to Jamshedpur to see the murals." Finley smiled. "I'm looking forward to those."

The *Khovar* and *Sohrai* murals in Jamshedpur were an attempt by industry and government to ensure the next generation both understood and engaged in keeping tribal traditions safe. The project involved panels on the railway station and along the highway leading into the industrial city that had been painted in traditional *Sohrai* images. Finley had seen photos of mothers and daughters painting, side by side, to preserve their culture. It was indeed that article, and her subsequent research, that had convinced her, and her editor, that there was more than just a short story here.

The support of *Traveler's Tales* had allowed her to focus exclusively on tribal arts while she was in India, rather than dividing her time between this story and shorter, more sellable subjects. She and Max had initially planned that she would research and write this project independently and then shop it around. She was freelancing so she could take her time and pursue the angles that mattered to her. This arrangement also allowed her to spend more time with Max. When Dan heard of it, however, those plans changed, and *Traveler's Tales* stepped in with money, but followed her timeline nonetheless.

To appease the publishing gods at the magazine, she had sent in a couple of *48 hours in . . .* pieces on Goa and Pondicherry, places she and Max had visited when they needed to get away from the noise of Delhi. Dan Burton, her editor and law school friend, was more than appreciative.

"Finley, you just saved me two hours of fast-talking and back-pedaling with the editorial board," Dan had said jokingly. "But you know how it is, always 'what have you done for me lately'—meaning in the last ten minutes."

He had again found her budget and consultant dollars that allowed her to pay Dr. Rao a small stipend in addition to covering his expenses. Dr. Rao was over the moon when she told him the amount of his stipend. In most cases, he agreed to act as a consultant without compensation because of his passion around the issue.

"Once we get the culture preservation story, we can wrap up this section and start weaving the individual artistic styles together into a larger cultural map of India." Finley handed the equipment bags to the driver, who in turn passed her another bottle of water.

Finley always felt like an Amazon next to Rao and Dev, their driver. She was almost a head taller and at least a stone heavier than the two of them. The sun had baked her a rich, nut brown, which provided a complementary canvas for her swamp-green eyes. She was not classically pretty like her mama and sister. She was what the British called "handsome," in their "always say something nice" kind of way.

"I will be so happy for a bath and a glass of wine tonight," Finley said. "Hope you don't mind if I beg off on dinner out. I think I'll have room service on the terrace tonight."

Dr. Rao hid his disappointment. "Certainly. It was exceedingly hot today. You must be very tired."

When the equipment was unloaded and secured in the hotel security office, Finley headed up to her room and Rao to his. The suites they occupied were more like corporate apartments than hotel rooms, with a bedroom and bath, small office space, living and dining area, and kitchenette. The hotel had a complete meal service and decent late-night dining options that ran until 11:00 p.m., for those days when traffic, either cars or cattle, stretched the trip back from the field well into the night.

She pulled out her computer and moved to the terrace to catch the setting sun. Without thinking about her movements, she pushed the speed dial button and settled in for her call.

4

"Hi. I was just thinking about you." Max's voice was low and husky when he answered the call. "I miss you. When are you coming home? Or should I come there?"

"I should be back in Delhi soon," Finley replied. "We have a couple more days of shooting, and then I think I can do the rest from there."

"Turn on your camera." Max had switched on his video so she could see his face. His beautiful face with the sleepy, teal blue eyes and the laugh lines that she ached to touch. His hair, dark curls that frequently flopped over one eye, had been tamed today, so his eyes were more prominent, more mesmerizing, more inviting.

"You don't want to see me just yet. I'm so dirty you should be able to smell me from there," Finley laughed. "Let me at least wash my face. I don't know what I was thinking, calling you before I cleaned up."

"I don't care. I just want to see you. Messy and all. Please," Max pleaded. "You know I love you, however you look. Just let me see your face."

Finley wavered a moment, then she clicked on the camera. He had seen her this sweaty before, but probably not this filthy. "Don't laugh!"

"You look gorgeous!" Max smiled his knowing smile that always gave her butterflies as his gaze traveled the full length of her face. She felt vulnerable and yet protected as he observed her. "You tired?"

"Exhausted. We've been working in over ninety-five-degree heat since six thirty this morning, but we got some good material. Both pictures and interviews. So, it was a good day. What about you?"

"Not bad. The data is slowly coming back in, and it's consistent with the other regions."

Max was running a large-scale effort for the Indian government, looking at health coverage and services for underserved communities in rural areas. He had been working on the project for almost a year and was hoping to conclude his findings in another couple of months.

"That's good news, right? It means you're on schedule to wrap up soon."

Finley's eyes traced the shape of his perfectly bowed lips and then proceeded to follow the tiny lines that were etched around his eyes. She wanted so badly to reach through the screen and feel the warmth of him. Instead, she brought herself back to the conversation.

"What're you doing for dinner?" Max asked, his eyes fixed on hers.

"Staying in, once I get a bath and a glass of wine," Finley said. "What about you?"

"Same. Rashmi fixed a large pot of curry last night, and I'm slowly working my way through it. It's your kind of spicy."

"Are you talking about my love of hot food or my personality?" Finley joked.

Max took his time answering. He gave a half laugh. "Both!"

"I'd better go get cleaned up before they have to fumigate this room," Finley sighed. "I just wanted to say hi."

"Hi to you, too. I miss you. See you in a few days." Max kissed his finger and placed it on the screen. "Love you."

"Love you, too," Finley whispered to a soon black screen.

Finley took her time in the bath. She wished her hair were shorter. The pixie cut she wore when she left Max in Morocco the first time would have been a lot cooler in this weather, but she knew Max loved her hair long, for whatever reason. She also liked her long, loppy curls—when they were clean and not heavy with sweat and dust.

Scrubbed and dried, she wrapped her still wet hair in a towel and padded into the kitchen to find wine. She poured herself a large glass of a dry white she had picked up in the liquor store. She hadn't expected the selection to be so extensive, but she found several European and Australian wines, and a few local ones, that her colleagues said were drinkable.

She grabbed a banana, the ripe sweetness catching in her nostrils, and sat at her desk, looking through her email backlog. Three quarters of the messages were deletable, but they were mixed in with the ones that would require careful reading and thought, so the weeding process was tedious. When her sister's face, with those piercingly clear green eyes, showed up on her phone, she had just finished sorting the last of the messages into the two categories. She switched off her computer and gave the phone her full attention.

"Okay, so how's it going? What are they like?" Finley asked, even before her sister said hello.

Her baby sister, S. Whittaker Blake, generally known as Whitt, had her future in-laws there in Tbilisi visiting. Whitt and David, her disarmingly handsome boyfriend, had recently come to an understanding on marriage. He had asked, and she had said yes—with a few caveats.

Ellie and Steve Quinn, David's parents, were in Georgia, seeing relatives on Ellie's side of the family, who were longstanding wine merchants in the region. It was that connection to wine through family that had drawn David into importing wines from this region into the US and Europe. He was now expanding to capture the rest of the ancient wine region and share their wines with the world. Having family in Georgia made it convenient for his parents to spend a week with their son and his soon-to-be bride.

"They're delightful. Mama and Daddy will like them a lot," Whitt said, referring to their own parents. "A little more laid back than Mama might be used to, but she'll adjust."

"They're from California, so what do you expect?"

"When they got into Tbilisi last week, they stayed with us for a few days, and then we all headed out to Kakheti, where they have the vineyards. Spectacular countryside."

"So, you got to meet the rest of the family, too?"

"Some of them I had met before. I mean, David has been here over two years, and we have been together for most of that time. I think that made being with his parents easier. I had more recent news than his mom did."

"She okay with that?"

7

"Yeah, she's pretty easygoing. They both are."

"So, this is going to work? I was waiting for a call from you saying you were running for the hills."

"It's all okay. Admittedly, I was nervous. I guess they were, too, but David put us right at ease. How did I get so lucky?"

"Well, baby sis, I'm glad you found him. In reality, he's the lucky one!"

"I think we both are." She continued, "How's it going with you? When do you head to Delhi? Is Max there or with you?"

"He's in Delhi, but he was here last week. Came to check in on the data gathering at a site not far from here and used Hazaribagh as his base."

Her phone vibrated, and Finley looked to see Mooney's blonde curls on her screen.

"It's Mooney. I'll just call her back after I am finished here."

"No, why don't you patch her in?" Whitt said. "I haven't talked to her in a while."

Whitt had met Mona Allen, otherwise known as Mooney, a few times over the years. She was Finley's best friend and had been a godsend when Finley needed a soft landing the first time she returned from Morocco. She and Max had had a profound misunderstanding that kept them apart for over three years and left both of them broken. It was a chance meeting during Finley's most recent trip to Morocco over a year ago that had repaired the rift and brought them together again.

"Moonster, what are you up to?" Whitt called into the phone before Finley had a chance to explain the three-way call.

"Whitt?" Mooney was confused. "Did I accidentally dial you instead of Finley?"

"Nope, we're all here." Finley flicked on her video again.

"What a great surprise!" Mooney's face lit up when Whitt appeared online.

"Whitt and I were talking and saw your call, so we decided to three-way it."

"Where are you guys?" Mooney asked. "I get whiplash trying to keep up with you."

"Finley is in Hazaribagh, in Jharkhand, and I'm still in Georgia."

When Whitt paused, Finley slyly dropped in the vital information. "With her future in-laws!"

Whitt quickly filled Mooney in on the parent meetings and family gatherings before getting the latest New York gossip. Mooney was the perfect channel for learning who of their friends was getting married, having a baby, in a relationship that was on the rocks, or seeing someone new.

"How's Max doing?" Mooney asked after she had finished filling the sisters in.

"He's fine. He's in Delhi. I just spoke to him. I'll head home in a few days."

Mooney smiled to hear Finley talk about wherever Max was as being home. For the longest time, she had feared that whatever had torn them apart would never be surfaced or resolved. It had pained her to see her friend suffer, but she learned in time that Finley wasn't the only one suffering. Max, too, had had to wrestle with demons when Finley left.

"So, you won't mind talking to me then, your dear old friend." Logan Reynolds popped his head into view. "Hello, Finley's sister. I'm Logan. I tried to make your sister love me, but she repeatedly rejected me for this fellow called Max. Lucky man."

Whitt had heard of Logan before. Very rich, very "sweet" according to Finley. And very FOF—"fond of Finley"—according to Mooney. Whitt now added a visual element—very handsome—to that description. Mooney had been trying, since Finley returned from Morocco the first time, to get the two of them together. Logan had seemed willing, but Finley always held back. The rediscovery of Max this last trip had thrown water on whatever might have sparked between the two of them.

"Logan, what are you doing bombing our video call?" Finley was laughing at the attractive, fawn-eyed visage sticking out the side of the camera view to block Mooney's face. *Leave it to Logan to have us laughing. He's indeed a good friend.*

"Thinking of coming to India. I have Challenger miles that I will lose on my jet package if I don't use them. India is within range," Logan said. "Would you and Max show me around if I came for a visit?"

Finley's eyes grew wide. *This man is serious. He is flying to India like other people might drive to the beach. Wealth does, indeed, have its privileges.*

"You know you're going to come whatever I say, so I might as well just concede defeat." Finley sighed. "I'll tell Max something."

"Does he know about us, darling?" Logan teased suggestively.

Finley raised an eyebrow and slowed her speech. "He's never even heard your name, you ninny."

"That will make it all the more interesting." Logan grinned cheekily. "Ciao, *bella*. See you in a couple of weeks."

DESPITE HIS USUALLY EASYGOING DEMEANOR, Max wasn't too thrilled about having Logan, whom he presumed to be a rival for Finley's affections, on the same continent, much less in the same city, as he. He listened quietly to Finley's explanation of the nature of her friendship with Logan. He didn't dispute her account, but he had his doubts. Why would the man be coming all the way to India if he didn't have a mission in mind? He sometimes wondered whether Finley was really as naïve as she seemed. Maybe it wasn't naïve as much as it was trusting.

He was glad that Whitt and David had arrived several days before for a visit. David's parents had left, and Whitt had been asked by the bank to begin preliminary conversations with the State Bank of India to lay the groundwork there for a microfinance program similar to the one she had launched in Georgia. David had decided to join her, having never been to India, and more importantly, not wanting to be away from Whitt for three weeks.

"How are you going to manage once we're married?" Whitt had asked David during one of the dinner gatherings of the Four

Musketeers, as they called themselves when they were together. "You recall that I live in Manila, not Tbilisi!"

David had just smiled in his easy, California way. "We'll figure it out. It'll all be good."

Finley got a fleeting mental image of her sister, in labor, stuck in traffic on the way to the hospital to deliver their first child and David smiling and saying, "It'll all be good." *You better pick your times to go chill on her, or she'll hand you your head on a platter.*

Finley was glad to have the foursome back together again. She had missed being with her sister these past few months. Video calls had their place, but nothing beat a heart-to-heart face-to-face. She noticed, too, that Max and David had developed a close bond that went beyond being supportive copartners to the two sisters. They seemed to genuinely value each other's friendship.

Logan had arrived only two days before, but already the temperature in the house had chilled. He smartly booked a room at the Imperial, even though Finley had offered to host him at their apartment.

"Finley, dearest, while Max calls it "our" house, collectively, it really is his house, and I know he doesn't want me there, polite as he is," Logan had said. "Are you sure he isn't English?"

The first meeting between the two had gone smoothly. Finley had been savvy enough to bring David and Whitt along to diffuse any pointed conversations. David was especially good in those situations. Logan had curbed his frequently irreverent tongue and played nice in the sandbox with Max, finding common ground over wines and single malts. He and David had bonded over kitesurfing, and Logan had admitted his ignorance of, but interest in, wines from the Caucasus.

The subsequent meetings had been brief or sightseeing related. The five of them had covered many of the key monuments in the city, taking in the Red Fort, a red-stone fortress built in 1618, Jama Masjid, India's largest mosque, and Gurudwara Bangla Sahib, a seventeenth-century Sikh house of worship, in one day. They had saved India Gate, a war memorial to the eighty thousand Indians lost in World War I, and Qutub Minar, a twelfth-century minaret, for the second day of sightseeing a couple of days later. Max and Whitt had to work, so Finley hired a driver and took David and Logan outside the city to these sights.

"I don't know if it's the lack of pollution or the sun or what, but the whites seem brighter here and the red stones deeper." Logan stood looking at the massive arch of India Gate, while Finley grabbed a few shots of the monument. She had at least one hundred frames of this building alone, one of the most popular sites in Delhi, but she always found another angle or light placement that warranted one more picture.

"I know. I spend so much of my time here trying to capture the intensity of color you can see with your eye but that somehow gets lost in pictures," Finley responded. "You have to see the Taj Mahal. The pictures just can't do it justice."

After lunch on the terrace at Dramz Delhi, the threesome headed to Qutub Minar, the tallest minaret in India and one of the oldest in the country. The structure and the surrounding buildings were some of the finest examples of early Islamic architecture, so much so that it was declared a UNESCO World Heritage site.

Exhausted at the end of the day, David and Finley labored up the front stairs to the apartment. Logan had appeared no better when they dropped him off at his hotel.

"You two looked like drowned rats." Whitt hurried to grab two bottles of water for the weary travelers.

Max laughed, watching Finley and David sigh after slipping off their shoes and cooling their feet on the marble tiles of the floor.

"Where did you go that has you so tuckered out?" Max asked. "Was the car not air-conditioned?"

"Yes, but the AC didn't reach to Qutub Minar." David leaned back on Whitt and let her mop his sweat-soaked brow with a cool cloth. "This heat is deadly. It just takes it out of you."

"And we did a lot of walking, too," Finley added. "I'm often in the heat at the site down south, but we aren't walking around in it."

"Will you recover enough for dinner out or shall we order in?" Max asked, looking at Finley's damp hair and haggard smile.

"We'll recover by then." David opened an eye and looked at Max. He was always hungry, and the prospect of missing a meal didn't sit well with him. Whitt laughed and patted his toned belly.

"We'll feed you, baby," she said. "Go hop in the shower and get changed."

It took Finley another ten minutes to pull herself off the sofa and into the shower. She was weary to the bone, and the cool created by the ceiling fans had made her sleepy. After a long, hot shower, she dried off and walked into the bedroom, where Max was lounging on the bed. He patted the space beside him and signaled her over. She snuggled next to him, comforted by his warmth and welcomed by his kiss to her forehead.

"Did you have a nice day?" he asked. "In spite of the heat."

"Yes. It was fun showing them around—and getting oriented in the city myself. There were parts of Delhi I had never seen before."

"What are you thinking of doing tomorrow? I have the weekend off, so I might be able to add a couple of days so we can have an extralong weekend."

"That would be nice. I'll ask David and Whitt what they are up for. Logan will gladly just tag along. Unless you would prefer that he find something else to do."

She looked up at Max, trying to gauge his mood. He was quiet for a few moments, clearly thinking. She prepared herself for the worst.

"No, he's welcome to join us," Max finally said. "He's your friend, after all."

The Four Musketeers had just returned from a sumptuous dinner at Saffron, an upscale pan-Indian restaurant not far from Max's apartment, and had settled into their after-dinner drinks, when Logan's face came up on Finley's phone.

"Hey, look. I just ran into someone I know from New York. He and his wife are heading to Jaipur for the weekend and invited us to join them. They're staying at the Rambaugh Palace," Logan said. "I offered them use of the plane. This weekend is on me if you guys can break free."

"Let me talk to the rest of the crew and get back to you." Finley looked at Whitt, twisting the cork of another bottle of champagne, and smiled. *That girl loves herself some champagne. Truth be told, I am not far behind.*

"Pour me some!" Finley begged her sister, as she clicked off her phone.

"Who was that?" Max's voice was measured, his eyes locked on her face. "Let me guess. Logan."

"Yes, he was inviting us to head to Jaipur for the weekend. A thank you for having been so gracious while he was here." Finley embellished a bit, judging it necessary by the look on Max's face.

Finley quietly added another bit of information. "And we get to take Logan's private jet."

Max's jaw flexed slightly when she said the words. Finley grabbed her glass of champagne and went to sit next to him. Her hand on his prompted his jaw to relax, and he smiled.

"I'll leave it to you. I should be able get away, and Jaipur is absolutely breathtaking." Max looked at Whitt and David as he spoke. "And it isn't every day we get to fly on a Challenger."

"I think you sold me. Assuming Whitt doesn't have anything keeping her here." David was almost begging her with his eyes to say yes.

He had heard so much about the Pink City and had been trying to figure out how to fit the Taj Mahal as well as a trip to Jaipur into an already packed schedule. The added bonus of a trip on a high-end private jet made it a once-in-a-lifetime opportunity.

"I don't have any meetings for the rest of our time here, so I'm fancy-free." Whitt shook her head at David's excitement. He flashed a smile as bright as California sunshine.

"So, I guess we're going to Jaipur. I'll shoot Logan a message and ask about logistics." Finley pulled out her phone and had started on the message when Max stilled her hand.

"But he doesn't need to cover the weekend," Max said, his voice firm.

"We'll leave that to you young bucks to fight out." Whitt directed her comment at Finley, but she cut a glance at Max. She understood his position, but she felt for her sister, who was caught in the middle. From what she had heard of Logan, he wanted to share his wealth, not flash it around. It was not unusual for him to pay other customers' grocery tabs on a whim or buy the whole bar a round, in addition to the sizeable checks his accountant wrote to local and global charities. From what Finley had said, he took joy from doing spontaneous acts of kindness.

Logan texted a suggested timeline, which included them meeting at the apartment and trailing each other to the hangar. He had booked two cars and drivers for the trip to the airport and for pickup in Jaipur. He indicated that rooms were already reserved, and the staff was awaiting their arrival.

Max had been inordinately quiet for the rest of the evening, while Whitt and David headed to their room to get packed. After throwing a random mix of casual and dressy outfits into a leather duffel, Finley brushed her teeth and slid into bed beside him. He looked up from his reading and then put the book aside.

"Are you sure you're okay with this?" She placed her hand on his arm, tracing the muscles of his forearm with her finger. "We don't have to go. We can send Whitt and David and just stay here."

Max put his arm around her shoulders and pulled her close. "It should be fun. We'll have a good time, I'm sure. Don't mind me. I'm just in a mood."

"Something you want to talk about?"

"Nothing that would make sense." He kissed her nose. "Let's get some sleep. We have an early morning tomorrow."

The car arrived exactly at six thirty for the thirty-minute trip to the airport. The morning was a clear one, with the hazy sunlight that marked sunrise in Delhi. While the streets weren't busy just yet, the city was already on the move with bicycles, handcarts, and trucks, all making early morning deliveries. Logan was waiting for them in front of their apartment building, the blue of his dark-washed jeans and linen jacket complementing the gray that streaked his hair. He greeted Whitt and Finley with a kiss before shaking hands with Max and David.

"I'm glad you all were up for an impromptu adventure. Sorry for the short notice," he remarked.

"No problem. Have bag, will travel." Max was trying hard to put himself in a good mood, or at least to fake it until he could. But Finley saw the jaw flex that signaled his real state of mind.

"Let me introduce you to my friends." Logan turned to greet the couple who had exited the car as the other bags were being put in the trunk. "This is Ravi Malhotra and his lovely wife, Devya. We know each other from New York."

A square man of medium height stepped forward to shake hands. He was impeccably dressed in a light-weight tweed jacket and slate-colored pants. It was hard to place his age, but Finley figured that he and Logan would be contemporaries in their early forties. If she had seen him in any other setting but this, she would have had him as a very wealthy Indian industrialist who most likely came from one of the "first" families. Which he probably was.

His wife, however, was another story. *Mama would have a good time with this one.* Finley sized her up as a beauty queen who had leveraged herself into a good marriage. Not that Finley had anything against beauty queens. She just had little time for smart women who chose to play dumb.

Devya Malhotra was clearly bored by the introductions and pleasantries. She rolled her eyes and tapped her lacquered nails against the polished finish of the car as the others talked about how Logan and Ravi had met and some of the business they had done together.

"Deyva, darling, why don't you get back in the car? I'm sure this sun is starting to get to you," her husband cooed, opening the door to usher her in. "We will be on our way in just a minute."

"How much longer?" Devya whined. "My dress is getting creased."

She flounced the skirt of a short-sleeved, brown and white polka-dot shirtdress that, despite the simplicity of the design, probably cost just shy of $1,000. She climbed back into the car, tapping her watch once she was seated.

"Not long," Ravi promised as he closed the car door. "We are almost ready."

Ravi's assessment of the timing was not far off. No sooner had Ravi closed the door for Devya than Logan and the others piled in. The drivers zipped through the backstreets of Delhi trying to beat the morning rush hour.

Finley had expected a sizeable plane when they rode up to the hangar and saw several jets lined up on the tarmac. However, she hadn't imagined anything quite as large as the plane she saw through the door that the driver had opened for her. It dwarfed the corporate jets she had flown on before. She prayed her mouth hadn't hung too far open.

"Welcome aboard!" Logan said as he led the way to the stairs. He stood aside to let his guests enter the cabin before coming up behind them.

The plane had seating for twelve, but the spaciousness suggested more could easily be accommodated. Every detail had been considered, from the sumptuousness of the buttery, hand-stitched leather on the seats to the match of the burled, pecan wood on the cabinetry. One felt as if they had entered an intimate private club rather than a mode of transportation.

"Hi, Linda," he acknowledged the comely flight attendant who was standing near the door. "I didn't know I would see you so soon, but thanks for making this little jaunt possible."

"No problem, sir. Once you're all settled, I'll take your drink orders. It's a very short flight this morning."

Despite the early hour, all Logan's guests accepted the suggestion of champagne. Finley and Max also asked for coffee. They shared a private laugh, each knowing the other would be hard-pressed to make it through the morning without a cup. Finley wondered what Whitt was planning on using for energy when she refused the coffee and went for another glass of champagne.

By the time they touched down, the sun was fully up, and Jaipur was bustling. Rickshaw drivers, buses, and motorbikes vied for a place on the already jammed streets. Vendors pushed their shutters back halfway to allow the light into their tiny stalls. School children in their blue and white uniforms lined the promenades on their way to class. Hawkers of all variety of foods were already braying for their first customers of the morning.

The Four Musketeers had kept each other company during the flight, while Logan and Ravi talked business. Devya rebuffed Whitt and Finley's attempts at small talk and stuck her nose in a series of fashion magazines. Her engagement with the others was no different when they arrived at the hotel.

The Rambaugh staff greeted the group like royalty, adorning each person's head with a dot of red powder and a necklace of marigold blossoms, while peacocks sauntered in and out of the open verandas. While Logan worked out the rooms, Finley and Max wandered the large, marble lobby, reading about the hotel's history.

The hotel and its opulent grounds, built in 1835, had been the residence of the Maharaja of Jaipur and his queen since 1925. In the early seventies, the Taj Hotels group purchased the palace and turned it into a luxury hotel. Queen Elizabeth, Jackie Kennedy, and Princess Diana had all walked the halls of the opulent building and grounds.

"This should be a very interesting weekend," Max whispered to Finley, when he spied Devya shooing the birds to catch a second glimpse of herself in one of the large decorative mirrors that graced the room. "The peacocks may have met their match."

3

NDICATIVE OF THE LEVEL OF hospitality it offered, the Rambaugh invited its newly arrived guests to coffee and pastries in the Polo Bar while their bags were being taken to their assigned rooms. Small clusters of guests gathered in the sports-themed clubroom. Mallets and polo shirts hung on the walls over gilded trophies, presumably belonging to the late Maharaja. The sweet smell of tobacco mixed with that of rich, dark-roasted coffee hung heavy in the air.

"This feels like a meeting of an English ladies gardening society or an English gentlemen's club," Whitt muttered under her breath as she reached for a cup of coffee. "I think we are the youngest ones here."

"You're probably right, but then again, this place requires money, and most folks are heading toward middle age before they make their first million," Finley said. "Logan just happened to be one who grabbed the golden ring early."

Max was intrigued. He had figured Logan had inherited his wealth rather than made it. "What did he make his money in?" he asked.

"Logistics. Don't ask me more than that," Finley responded. "He came up with some logistics software that made him a mint when he was thirty."

"Impressive," was all Max said.

As expected, David spied the pastries and went to investigate, dragging Whitt and Max with him. Finley took advantage of the solitary moment to survey the room and the other guests. Some she had spoken to in the lobby when they were checking in. Others she had introduced herself to as she made her way over to the table for her third cup of coffee. Whitt was right. This was an older crowd, but there was a sprinkling of guests that were under forty.

"How did you get roped into coming here?" An attractive young woman in her early thirties had sidled up to Finley and joined her in the dual art of coffee sipping and people watching. "I think most of them will be on oxygen by dinner time."

Finley stifled a laugh before answering, her eyes still focused on the crowd. "A friend from New York. And you?"

"My parents. The older couple over there." The young woman nodded toward a pair of beige, linen-upholstered barrel chairs in which sat a handsome, middle-aged gentleman with a lavish white moustache and a beautiful, chisel-featured woman in an elaborately woven sari. Finley could see the resemblance between the two women as soon as she glanced at the woman beside her. The deep-set, doe-shaped eyes, the artfully shaped nose, and the elegant neck tagged them as family.

"Is there a particular occasion, or just a break away from Delhi?" Finley asked.

"My father just retired from the university. My mother and I figured we'd better grab him while we can." The young woman laughed a deep, throaty laugh that seemed almost too old for her. "He has already accepted so many speaking engagements, my mother had to hire an assistant to keep his calendar straight."

"Was he a professor?" Finley turned her full attention to the young woman.

"Yes, dean of the fine arts department at the university in Delhi. He specialized in Mughal art."

"Fascinating," Finley said.

"What is fascinating?" Max had walked up behind her and put his hand on her waist. She caught his hand and wrapped his arm in hers.

"Her father, the gentleman over there, is an expert in Mughal art," Finley smiled at the young woman standing beside her. "I have done it again. Carried on a rather lengthy conversation with someone whom I can't even introduce, because I don't know their name. I'm Finley Blake. And this is Max—Max Davies."

"I am equally guilty. I am Hema Gupta. And my parents are Drs. Arvind and Neeta Gupta," the woman announced.

"What is your mother's discipline?" Max asked.

"Anthropology. And no, I got none of their braininess," Hema said, smiling.

"What do you do?" Finley was dying to know what her newly found partner in cattiness did for a living. She suspected she might be a journalist or a fashion designer, the former because of her observation skills, the latter because of the trendy stilettos she was wearing.

"A radiologist," Hema related matter-of-factly.

"Not too shabby. Why do you contend you aren't brainy? I thought doctors were among the best and brightest," Max inquired.

"Not in India. Here, they are a dime a dozen," Hema laughed. "I don't mind it. I like my work. And what do you do?"

Max and Finley briefly described their projects and what brought them to India. It had sounded so well thought-out, when in reality, it was anything but. Finley was here because Max was here. Yes, the tribal mural project was likely to get her recognition in certain circles, but that wasn't what had drawn her to India. It was Max who was her sole reason for being here.

"What do you know of any of the other guests?" Finley directed Hema back to their conspiracy of gossip, which had bonded them in the first place.

"The woman over there, dripping in jewels, is Sandra Ruiter. South African. Seems to have brought half the mines with her when she came over." Max failed to suppress a laugh, so he masked it as a cough. "A recent widow whose husband left her *very* wealthy. Doing a trip to Jaipur was on their bucket list."

Hema continued, "The young couple standing near the window are from Dubai or somewhere in the UAE. He's in commercial real estate, she is a stay-at-home mum with two children, who are almost school-age. I think their name is Zaheri, but don't quote me on that."

Finley's eyes pivoted from Sandra Ruiter to the well-dressed couple holding hands and watching the peacocks through the large window. She suspected they were celebrating something special from the way they looked at each other. And the way the woman kept fingering the large stones in her necklace.

"And finally, there is Elise, Mrs. Kenneth Boyd-Hampton, as she refers to herself. Very rich, very aloof. She isn't one to mingle with the riffraff, if you know what I mean," Hema raised her hand as if drinking from a glass. "And I think, very pickled."

Finley met the gesture with a knowing nod.

"You've been very busy!" Max arched his eyebrow at the young woman's thorough descriptions.

"We got here almost two hours ago. Our luggage was delayed coming from the airport." Hema smiled. "There wasn't much else to do."

She put down her coffee cup and started toward where her parents were now standing. "Looks like there is movement. Our bags must have arrived. Nice meeting you. I'm sure I'll see you around."

Max turned Finley in his arms after Hema had left. "So, what's the plan for today, or has it been decided?"

"I haven't the slightest idea. Logan has been occupied with Ravi since we arrived, and I haven't talked to Whitt or David," she said. "Is there anything in particular you wanted to do? I saw you looking at Whitt's guidebook."

"Nope. Nothing in particular. We can just wander downtown today and save whatever more formal touring we're going to do until tomorrow and the next day." Max looked out at the stretch of manicured lawn leading to more formal gardens. "I'm also fine just walking around here. Whatever is your pleasure, madame."

"I'm easy, too. I know Whitt is going to want to tour, so whatever they do, we can tag along with, if that is okay with you?"

Within minutes, the guests were escorted to their rooms by a stiffly uniformed bellman. Whitt and David were next door to Max and Finley in a ground floor suite that looked onto the lattice-tiled center courtyard. The room itself was tastefully appointed in what Finley called Mughal style—richly colored brocade curtains and bed coverings, intricately patterned silk rugs, fringe-ringed ottomans and tufted chairs, and stately portraits of the Maharaja and his wife in various poses.

On the floor in the sitting room and bedroom, the staff had crafted an elaborately designed, paisley patterned *rangoli* made of golden marigold and dark-pink rose petals. The room smelled of marigold and white roses, the latter of which were arranged into elegant puffs of white and green and placed in the bay windows that looked out onto courtyard.

"All right, I'm impressed." Max stood in the entry between the sitting room and the bedroom, taking in the minute details that made the room tasteful rather than overdone. "I can't even pretend to be jaded."

Finley had to agree. The design had been carefully executed to reflect the majestic proportions of the building and its architecture and yet still be welcoming to guests. She suspected the service would fill in any gaps.

She opened her duffle that had been placed on the luggage rack and began to unpack the clothes she had haphazardly shoved into the bag late last night.

"I'm going to have to get most of this steamed out." Finley shook a dress and jumpsuit as if that would iron out the wrinkles. "I should have taken a bit more care in packing."

"I'm sure they can get someone to take care of that for you," Max said. "In fact, I'll bet if you think on it hard enough, a little genie will come out of the woodwork and, without a word, make it so."

"Can you imagine having this as your ordinary life?" Finley flopped onto the bed and kicked off her shoes.

"Nope, but I suppose I could get used to it," Max joined her on the bed and pulled her close.

"So, Logan is growing on you?" she asked.

"I wouldn't go that far, but he isn't a bad guy." Max gave Finley a side glance. "As long as he doesn't move in on my girl!"

Finley gave his arm a playful punch. "I told you, he's just a friend. F-r-i-e-n-d. Period. The end."

"So you say." Max managed to escape her reach this time by answering the knock on the door.

Whitt and David walked in, gave the room a once-over, and sat down on the sitting room sofa.

"Your room and ours have a similar layout, just different colors," David reported before repeating Max's words of only minutes before. "I could get used to this."

"I bet you could!" Whitt kidded. "So, what's the deal for today?"

Finley looked at Max, who recounted their earlier conversation. "Basically, we're going with the flow."

Whitt watched her sister pull on a pair of black-and-white patterned wedge sandals. "That's a fun combination—those shoes with the mustard wrap dress. I wouldn't have paired them together, but it works."

Whitt shifted her attention back to the conversation about the day's schedule. "I heard some talk about heading into town. We supposedly have the cars for the time that we're here, so we can go anywhere."

"Including shopping?" Finley asked.

Finley knew her sister. If there was shopping to be had, she would find it. And she now had David back as her trusty shopping bag carrier. Finley smiled, thinking about their time in Morocco, when David, new to his relationship with Whitt, had played the role of porter without complaint.

"Well, I might know of a few places that are worth swinging by."

David merely smiled and took her hand in his. "Yes, dear."

"Let's get out of here before I hurl!" Max joked and headed for the door.

In the lobby, they found Logan lounging on a divan of hushed-gold silk, phone in hand. He recalled wealthy pooh-bahs of old. He looked up when they walked in.

"I was just texting you. Do you guys have plans for the day?" He stood expectantly in front of Finley, who was standing with her arm locked through Max's.

"Nope, we were just talking about options. We're pretty much open." She smiled, knowing the answer before she asked the question, "Do you have ideas?"

"Ravi is going to stay with Devya. She isn't up for touring. He said he'll see us at polo on Sunday, if not before. There's some sort of match to which all guests are invited," Logan said. "Anyway, I struck up a conversation with Sandra while we were waiting in the Polo Bar, and she mentioned that she is game for heading downtown. One of our drivers, Vik, offered to take us around to Hawa Mahal and the City Palace. We'll just take two cars."

"Sounds like a plan to me," Whitt concurred. Turning to see Sandra approach, Whitt looked slightly puzzled and asked under her breath, "Is she going like that—with all that jewelry?"

Sandra, who looked to be well-preserved, somewhere in her fifties, was wearing a flowy, flowered jumpsuit and bejeweled flats, which matched the ropes of gold and semiprecious stones that circled her neck. Whitt watched in silence as she made her way across the room. *That is an accident waiting to happen. If she doesn't slip on the cobbles in those shoes, she will trip on that flouncy getup she is wearing. That will make it real easy for pickpockets to slip those chains off her neck and be gone before she can even cry for help.*

26

"Hello, and who is this charming group of travelers?" Sandra asked in a South African lilt. She waited for Logan to make the introductions, which he dispatched quickly, until he got to Finley, whom he had saved for last.

"And this is Finley, my dear friend from New York." Logan pointedly turned to Max, who was flanking Finley. "I thought I had her ensnared until this guy came along and carried her away."

Finley smiled nervously and waited for Max's reaction.

"Sorry, old man," Max gave Logan a sly half smile. "Not!"

Logan laughed at the jab and took Sandra's arm to lead her out to the waiting cars. "I will escort this lovely lady, and you can follow in the other car. Unless one of you wants to come with us."

"No, we'll be fine packed in here." Whitt slid into the back seat.

Darsh, their driver, gave the group a guided tour of the sights and sounds of the city as they inched their way through traffic.

"Jaipur is a relatively new city in the Indian timeline, coming as a planned city in the early 1700s. We have a population of over three million people, making us one of the most populous cities in India," he explained as he navigated the congestion.

All the while, bicycles wove their way around cars, trucks, and pedestrians, using their hands to push off diesel-belching buses. Women balanced babies, satchels, and groceries on the motor-bikes that snaked through the jammed traffic. Men carried flats of bricks and bags of cement on their heads through the streets and between the cars before climbing rickety scaffolding to the final construction site.

"Is it always this crowded?" David asked as he craned his neck to catch the thousand bits of action playing out in the live movie in front of him.

"Most of the time, except early morning and late at night," Darsh admitted. "The streets in the old part of town were made for donkey carts and a few people. Now we have cars and buses and too many people."

"The Hawa Mahal was built in the late 1700s by one of the maharajas based on an old palace in one of the provinces that had a honeycombed façade. The latticework was designed to allow the women of the palace a view of the outside world without being seen, but it also helps with cooling the palace." Darsh pointed to the iconic, earthen-blushed, wedding-cake-looking building that they passed on their left. "This is actually the back of the palace, not the front. There is some good shopping back behind this street, if you are interested."

Whitt sat up a bit straighter, scanning the crowded arcades for shops worth coming back to. "If we have time for a quick stop. By the way, do you know of the Agarwal textile shop? I was told they have lovely rugs and pashminas."

"Yes, I know them. They also have good jewelry upstairs," Darsh replied. "We can go after the City Palace."

Tucked inside a stone courtyard, like a little package that was carefully guarded, the City Palace sat in the middle of a large, cobblestoned plaza. The red-stone building was built on the site of a royal hunting lodge, and its history and the city of Jaipur were closely linked. The complex had several pavilions, courtyards, gardens, and temples and was designed to be at the center of the growing city.

"That little balcony"—Darsh pointed to an enclosed loge that extended out several feet from the face of the building—"was where the women who were sequestered in purdah watched for visitors or the maharajah's return from his travels."

The tour of the palace took the rest of the morning and the early part of the afternoon. David was enchanted by the Mughal and Rajput architecture that made the red and white stone buildings look like a gingerbread and icing masterpiece. After hearing the earlier mention of purdah, Max peppered Vik and Darsh with questions about the region under the maharaja's dominion and the ways of life at the time.

As they talked, Finley wandered the stone walkways, her camera in hand. She focused on catching shadows and shards of light as they played against the deep-colored walls. What struck her was the crispness that the dry air and sun in Jaipur gave images. She took the time to try a range of different filters, shooting the same image multiple times to see the effect. To be a master of anything, one must always be a student, her daddy had told her once when she was young. *I am nowhere near a master, but every new location makes me a student again.*

"What are you seeing?" Max stood next to her, watching her switch out a filter and start shooting again.

"Everything and nothing," Finley laughed. "Sometimes I don't know what I have until after I get home. I just keep shooting because I'm afraid that I'll miss something if I try to find it before I click. Crazy, huh?"

"Not at all." Max reached over to brush an errant curl from her eyes. "You've captured some spectacular sights with that method."

She looked up at him and smiled. She knew what serendipity and a camera could do. She remembered well the suspended animation of an elephant spraying water above its head in Sri Lanka, the Mondrianesque shots of the buildings in the Casablanca medina, and the numerous pictures of women and children whose boldness, or shyness, lent humanity to her photographs.

"You guys almost finished? I don't want to hold you up with my incessant picture taking," Finley asked.

"Whenever you are. I think Vik and Darsh have talked themselves out. And David is hungry."

"Go figure!" Finley knew David's constant need for food and wondered how he managed to eat so much and stay so fit. *Good genes. Between Whitt and David, their babies are going to have next to no body fat. If I ever have kids, mine will probably be pudge balls.*

Vik led the group a short way outside the palace gates to a small restaurant that melded old-world charm with modern design. The group settled into an outdoor banquette that was bookended by large stone arches. They had the place to themselves, shielded from the noise and crowd of the rest of Jaipur by high walls and shade trees. Finley wondered what a life shut away from the outside world, with only the daily requirements of court life as a measure of time, would have been like. *Like any life. Once you get used to it, it's yours. It's all that you know, so it becomes normal. Like Whitt with David, and me with Max. It just is.*

They let Vik and Darsh order for them and then sat back and waited for the feast to begin. First came the *pakoras, dal batti,* a local wheat flour dumpling eaten with a red lentil dal, and *aloo chaat,* a potato-based dish topped with chutney. This was followed by a mutton curry and grilled vegetables with rice. Finally, the waiter brought an assortment of dessert samplers including *churma,* sweet balls of flour, jaggery, and cardamom, *ghewar,* a honeycomb-like confection, and *mawa kachoris,* a fried pastry stuffed with milk curd and nuts and dipped in sugar syrup. In time, even David was begging for the food parade to stop.

"Don't forget that there is afternoon tea and then drinks on the terrace tonight," Sandra said. "There's going to be a palm reader, too."

Finley shuddered at the prospect of more food. She took the time to look around the table. The slower pace of lunch had given the group time to learn a lot about each other. Logan was a skillful conversation master. He knew how to draw out a diversity and richness of thought that wasn't evident from the cocktail debates he had orchestrated over drinks with Mooney and her crowd.

At Cork, he had, at times, come across as self-absorbed, business-focused, and frivolous. Here, he had depth and a genuine curiosity that made others want to share. He drew Sandra out on the recent death of her husband and the loss she experienced. He got Finley talking about what she felt when she got behind the lens. He even got Whitt to say out loud that she wanted kids and Max to consider getting a puppy when his life became less transient.

"And what about you, Logan?" Max asked, as the last of the wine was being poured. "What is it that makes you tick?"

"Simple. Using what I have to make the people I care about smile," Logan replied, his eyes drifting over to and resting on Finley.

4

BY THE TIME THEY RETURNED to the hotel, just before teatime, Whitt and Sandra had added substantial acquisitions to their jewel cache. Their stop at Agarwal's had Whitt and Sandra jumping for joy. While Whitt was judicious in her selections, Sandra was ready to buy the store and its excess inventory. And Logan stood ready to help her. She purchased handfuls of premade necklaces and rings before asking how long it would take to have a commissioned piece made. In the meantime, Finley sorted through cashmere pashminas, while Max perused the rugs.

"You aren't interested in the jewelry?" Max asked after buying Finley a peacock blue shawl with intricate embroidery.

"No, goodness. I can barely wear the pieces I have." Finley looked over at her sister and David, who was helping Whitt decide between two bracelets. "That is Whitt's domain, not mine."

Max took advantage of their sheltered position, away from the rest of the group, to sneak a kiss. He held her close and kissed her thoroughly, leaving her a little light-headed. When they pulled apart, he raised her hands to his lips and kissed each of her fingers in turn.

"Thank you, but what brought that on?" Finley stepped back to see him fully.

"Just an overwhelming need to let you know how much I love you." He moved in to whisper in her ear.

Finley met his eyes and said quietly, "I love you, too."

"So, what did you guys get?" Whitt had wandered over and found them behind a stack of scarves and textile hangings.

"We selected a rug that will be delivered to us in Delhi next week, and Finley got another pashmina," Max said.

"Well, I think these ladies are shopped out and ready for tea, if we're set to head back," Logan related jovially, having followed Whitt and David to where Finley and Max were standing.

When they wandered back to the cars, Logan hung back slightly to allow himself to be paired with Finley walking down the narrow path that led to the parking lot. "Are you having a good time? You're awfully quiet at times, so it's hard for me to tell."

"We're having a blast. Thanks so much for the invitation and making all the arrangements." Finley stopped to plant a kiss on his cheek before hurrying to catch up to the rest of the group. "You are a dear."

Finley and Max barely had time to drop their bags in the room and wash their faces before Whitt and David were knocking on their door.

"What's taking you guys so long?" David smirked, his eyebrow raised. "No midday hanky-panky, I hope."

Finley laughed. "No, I just think your second stomach is calling you. Good gracious, you can eat!"

"You can say that again," Whitt smiled. "I don't know where he puts it."

"I'm just a growing boy," David laughed.

He was already out on the long veranda that ran in front of the rooms and was heading to the terrace where the staff was serving tea. The center table on the terraces was stacked with layer upon layer of scones, cakes, finger sandwiches, and tarts. From this elaborate display of tea fare, the staff was arranging tiered serving stands for each of the tables.

The Four Musketeers chose a large, round table farthest from the hustle of the confection station and closest to the gardens. From there, they could see the reflecting pools and the peahens and their mates strutting across the expansive lawns.

"This is simply spectacular!" Finley took in the acres of green space and quiet in the middle of a major metropolis. "Look at the castle on the hill. Does anyone know which fort that is?"

"I think it is Nahargarh. If I remember correctly, it'll be lit up later tonight." Whitt wished she had stuck her guidebook in her satchel. "We can ask our waitress when she comes."

David had already taken care of having a bottle of champagne iced for Whitt. She smiled appreciatively when the waitress brought flutes over without a word from anyone at the table.

"You look after me so well!" She kissed David's cheek.

"We have to remember to ask them to add extra smoked salmon sandwiches to our platter." David recalled an afternoon tea in Sri Lanka not long ago, during which Whitt and Max had inhaled a full plate of sandwiches between the two of them.

"As long as I get my tarts!" Finley said.

"May we join you?" Logan approached the table, flanked by Sandra, who wore a necklace with a sizable emerald in the center surrounded by smaller stones that matched her blouse, and another woman, to whom the group had not been introduced.

"Certainly." Max began to add chairs to make space for the new additions.

"Elise Boyd-Hampton," the new addition intoned, making her way around the group. Like Sandra, she too had on significant jewelry—a cabochon, pigeon blood ruby pendant. "So how do you all know each other?"

Whitt explained the range of relationships around the table. Whitt noticed Logan's cheek twitch slightly when she introduced Max as Finley's boyfriend. *He likes the girl. Does he think he still has a chance? This is more interesting than I thought. I wonder if Finley knows. Probably not. So much for "friends."*

"And what brings you to Jaipur?" Max asked Elise, who was explaining to the waitress how she liked her gin and tonic.

"Sorry to be so particular, but I find if you are explicit at the outset, by the end of your visit, they generally get it right." There was an air of condescension in her tone that Finley found off-putting.

Elise continued, "I came for the adventure. I call Cape Town home, but I am never there. I divide my time between London and Ibiza, and I was getting bored."

"How long will you be in Jaipur then?" Finley asked. She realized that she grew impatient with people who got bored easily. *There is so much need in the world. For God's sake, make yourself useful.*

"Until I get bored again! I have a driver, and we'll take a few side trips to Jodhpur and the Taj. And wherever else we can think of. We are looking into the tigers at Ranthambore. We'll see." She took the first sip of her gin and tonic and nodded.

The size of the group lent itself to smaller conversations and soon the group began talking to each other in clusters of two or three at a time. Whitt and David sat together, hands entwined. Max had settled in across the table from Whitt and David, with Elise and Sandra on either side. Somehow, he had gotten separated from Finley when Logan and his entourage joined the table. He now glowered at Logan and Finley, who sat side by side, heads together, whispering and laughing, while he struggled to make polite conversation with the two older ladies.

After a while, Logan turned to Sandra and began a conversation that soon included the full table.

"The hotel said that they could arrange tickets to Jal Mahal and Amber Fort tomorrow if we wanted to go," Sandra announced. "I think they do the lake trip in the morning, with a stop at some fort in between, then the afternoon at Amber Fort."

"Is that the place with the elephants?" Elise asked. "I had better lay off the G&Ts or I'll go sliding off." She cut a sly glance at Max. "But I'm sure this dashing gentleman will come to my aid."

Max blushed in spite of himself and looked at Finley to save him.

"Max is indeed quite gallant. You needn't worry." Finley smiled at Elise's boldness.

She liked seeing Max a little off-balance. He was always so buttoned-up, so in control, that seeing him flustered by Elise's flirtation was endearing. She tried to catch his eye to assure him that it was all in good fun, but he had already turned his attention to Sandra and was engaged in conversation.

Drinks and dinner ended up being a continuation of the same conversation. The group decided against getting dressed for a proper dinner in the restaurant and instead ordered more champagne—and gin and tonics for Elise—and a mix of appetizers from the à la carte menu.

After dinner, David cornered Max and suggested a nightcap at the bar. Sensing the need for a man-to-man, Finley and Whitt headed off to Whitt's room after bidding the rest of the group goodnight. Logan promised to escort Sandra and Elise to their rooms before grabbing a drink with Ravi in the bar.

"I hope Elise and Sandra start hanging out together. Both seem a little lonely." Whitt had tucked her feet under her on the sofa in the sitting room, while Finley had claimed the comfy side chair beside her. The waiter had delivered the rest of the opened bottle of champagne to the room with two clean flutes and a small plate of madeleines and chocolates.

"If they feed us anymore, I'm going to burst!" Finley exclaimed. "David can have my chocolates and madeleines."

"I'm sure he'll appreciate that." Whitt turned to her sister with a conspiratorial gleam in her eye. "So, who do you think did it?"

She was starting a round of the Murder Game, a story-building diversion that the girls had thought up as children to keep themselves occupied during their parents' travels around the world. The object of the game was to include their fellow travelers in sordid tales of death and deception. Many a morning had seen them giggling uncontrollably upon sighting one of the guests that they had

35

implicated in drunken drama, financial finaglings, or titillating temptation.

"Who died and how?" Finley asked, taking a sip of her champagne.

"Sandra. Strangled with a rope of pearls," Whitt replied.

"I think it was an accident or a robbery gone wrong."

Whitt measured out the remaining champagne. "You of little imagination. I think it was Elise, whose husband, years ago, had an affair with Sandra. It's clear there is little love lost between the two of them, and yet they tour together."

"I think they tour together so that they can hang out with Logan. He charms them." Finley smiled at the image of her friend catering to every need of the two women. *He is a special person. He looks after everyone so well. I hope he finds someone to look after him.*

"Ever the practical one." Whitt was clearly disappointed that the game hadn't resulted in a juicier conclusion. "Let's call Charlie, since the guys aren't here. She wants to hear about the in-laws, and we haven't found time to connect. It's only around midnight in Manila, but Charlie will definitely still be up."

Finley had never met Charlie, Whitt's running buddy in Manila, but she had heard a lot about her. Née Charlotte Larson, Charlie had come to Manila from Seattle to open and run one of the first no-kill shelters in the country. She had taught English in South Korea straight out of college and always used to go diving in the Philippines during break. It was on these trips that she began to see the desperate need for animal shelters in the Philippines. Vet school and a few other gigs in animal shelters around the US had brought her full circle and back to the Philippines.

"Hey, you, what're you up to?" Whitt questioned when Charlie came online. "You finally get to meet my sister. How this never happened before is beyond me!"

"Hi, Charlie! So glad to finally meet you." Finley watched as the petite, ginger-headed sprite on the screen adjusted the angle of the camera on her computer. Whitt had said Charlie had just turned thirty, but the woman on the screen, in her jeans and powder blue T-shirt, barely looked older than twenty-one.

"You're telling me. You would think that Whitt was purposely trying to keep us apart," Charlie laughed. "I was beginning to think she really didn't have a sister."

"I know. After the third glass of champagne, she has been known to hallucinate," Finley joked.

"You two need to stop ragging on me if you want to hear any of my future in-law stories!" Whitt looked at Charlie and leveled the mock threat.

For the next hour, Whitt had Finley and Charlie holding their sides in laughter at some of the situations she had found herself in while David's parents were in Georgia. When Whitt had recounted the visit to Finley earlier, it had seemed pretty cut-and-dried. Egged on by Charlie, the stories grew more elaborate and exaggerated. Finley was glad that her sister had found a friend with whom she had common interests and who shared a similar worldview. Life as an expat could be lonely without it.

"I hope the guys are having as much fun as we are," Whitt pondered. "David seemed rather serious when he mentioned drinks to Max. Do you know if something is up?"

Finley shook her head. All she knew was that the guys were having after-dinner drinks.

Max was on his second single malt before David got to the point. He had seemed nervous, uncomfortable. So much so that Max had wondered whether he had done something to upset him—or Whitt, for that matter. Then he began to wonder if Whitt had put him up to asking Max some pointed questions about his relationship with Finley.

He couldn't blame her if Whitt had indeed sent David on an exploratory mission. He knew the questions would come at some point. He and Finley had been together more than three years—with over three years of separation in between the first two years and the last, most glorious year. Far longer than Whitt and David had been together. And yet it was they, not he and Finley, who were getting married.

If the questions came, he didn't know that he could answer. Not because he had something to hide but because he himself didn't know the answers. He knew that he had been distant at times with Finley and that he sometimes confused her with his moods. But there was so much unresolved. So much he was trying so hard to sort through.

"Are you excited about getting married?" Max finally decided he needed to say something to open the door to the reason for their meeting.

"Yeah, but I haven't formally asked her yet." David watched as Max's brow knitted in confusion.

David knew that everyone was acting as if it was a done deal. In fact, he was as well. But the truth was that he hadn't gotten down on one knee and popped the question. He would, though. Soon.

"I'm not sure I understand." Max tried to process what he had just heard.

"Whitt isn't like most women, where you pop the question and you get a straight answer," David started. "At least on things like marriage, she has to cogitate on it." He continued, "For me, it was a pretty clear shot. 'Whitt, I want to marry you. Will you marry me?' But for her, it's taken longer."

"But she did say yes. Right?" Max was still struggling to make sense of this. He had his own view of marriage and its complications. He wondered whether Whitt had the same reticence.

"Yes. She had some conditions that were easy for me to agree to," David said with a half laugh. "But because of that, because she took time to settle into it, I never got around to the picture-perfect ask."

"So, what does this mean? I mean, I think Whitt's mother is deep into wedding planning."

"Oh, so am I! Whitt, not so much, but she'll get into when it's about the ring and the dress and the right champagnes." David straightened in his chair and directed his full attention to Max, who seemed increasingly confused. "That's what I wanted to ask you about. Without Whitt and Finley around. Would you be my best man?"

Max paused for a few stunned seconds before bursting into a hearty laugh. He stood and shook David's hand before wrapping him in a hug. "I would be honored. Truly honored. Are you sure there isn't a university friend or travel buddy you'd rather ask? I just want to be sure."

"No, I've come to respect and admire you over the past year or so. I really value you as a friend, and I want you to stand with me when I marry that crazy woman . . . *my* crazy woman." David shrugged and waited for Max's confirmation.

"Well then, you have found your best man! I really am honored."

The two drank in silence for a few minutes, each deep in their own thoughts. It was late, but neither of them made a move to leave.

David broke the silence. "Any thoughts about you and Finley—"

Before he could finish the thought, staff started running toward the stairwell beside the Polo Club. David signed the bill quickly, and he and Max followed the crowd to find out what all the commotion was about. At the edge of the crowd, they saw Logan and Ravi.

"What's going on?" Max asked the two men.

"Seems like one of the staff took ill. One of the young houseboys," Logan reported, straining to see what was happening.

His height gave him some advantage. He could see a small form, immobile, on the staircase. It appeared to be a boy, not more than twelve or thirteen. He was in his uniform—starched white kurta, matching pajamas, and black felt shoes.

"He's dead!" one of the waitresses screamed hysterically. "He's dead! He has gone with the gods! He's dead!"

A large man in a gray pinstripe suit pushed his way through the crowd, clapping his hands to scatter the assembled. "Let me through! Sanjay, Dev, you stay to help me. The rest of you, please return to your duties."

He turned to the remaining crowd, mainly guests who stood staring at the prone figure on the floor. "I am Veer Patel, resident manager here. One of our staff appears to have fallen ill. We will take him to his quarters and send for the doctor. Please return to your activities. We have this under control."

Logan and Ravi turned to head back to the bar. They nodded in passing at Max and David, who watched the manager pick up the slender boy and carry him down the path that ran behind the main building.

"That's unfortunate. Such a young kid," David said. "I hope he's all right."

"Indeed." Max sighed softly. "I think I'm going to turn in. That was more excitement than I needed."

He reached to shake David's hand again, his smile wide. "I truly am honored."

"WHAT'S GOING ON OUT THERE?" Finley met Max at the door.

"One of the houseboys took ill or got hurt. It wasn't clear which." Max looked done in. He headed to the bathroom to wash his face. He came to the bedroom door wiping the water out of his eyes with a hand towel, which he ran over his hair quickly. Soft, wet curls hid his eyes until he brushed them back with his fingers. "It looked pretty bad."

"That's awful. I hope he's all right." Finley climbed back onto her side of the bed and picked up her book. "Before that happened, did you and David have a nice evening? Whitt and I called Charlie, her friend in Manila. She's a hoot."

She wasn't really interested in reading. The book just provided her with something to do to fill in the pauses that were becoming more prevalent in her conversations with Max. He had said he was working some things through, and she wanted to give him space, but sometimes the silences were long and awkward, like making small talk with a stranger.

"Yeah. It was good." The rest of the thought hung in the air. Max grabbed his sweatpants and Yale T-shirt from behind the bathroom door and sat on the edge of the bed as he changed.

"You guys were gone quite a while. You just shooting the breeze or plotting world domination?" She was grabbing at straws now. She didn't know why it mattered to her what they had talked about, but somehow it did.

Max smiled at the absurdity of her statement, kissed her nose, and switched off the light. "Good night."

Breakfast the next morning was a morose affair. The staff was still reeling from the news that the young boy, Ajai, had not recovered from whatever his ailment or injury was. Rumors about the cause were rampant. Some said that he was bitten by a snake. Another theory had him dying of a heart attack. No formal statement was made by management and so the stories filled in the gaps.

The weather was pleasant, a cerulean sky scattered with feathered clouds that kept the sun from getting too hot. As such, most of the guests had chosen to sit outside on the terrace. Max and Finley nodded to Hema and her parents on their way to the table where Logan and David sat over breakfast.

"Where's Whitt?" Finley wondered if her sister were ill or if she and David had argued.

"She just went to get a hat since she refuses to wear sunglasses." David looked up at Finley's sunglasses knowingly.

Finley laughed. "She isn't going to change. She never has, and never will, wear the things. And I can't live without them."

"What do they have that looks good?" Max moved his glance from Logan's and David's plates to the buffet that was laid out under the veranda.

"You name it they have it," David said.

"And you're going to eat it!" Whitt planted a kiss on his lips and slipped into the seat between David and Logan. "Did you get me some coffee?"

David pointed to the small porcelain pot at the top of her place setting. "Do you want me to pour you a cup?"

"Please, if you don't mind." Whitt touched his hand to signal her request. She had closed her eyes and pulled the sun hat low on her head.

Finley paused before sitting down fully. She searched her sister's face, trying to discern the reason for her sister's pallor and apparent queasiness. *Good God, don't let her be pregnant. Mama would die of mortification!*

"You okay?" Finley finally asked. "You're looking a little peaked."

"I think I got a bit dehydrated," Whitt said. "The sun is already really hot today, and we took a walk around the grounds early this morning."

"You should probably switch to tea, then. Coffee will only make you more parched," Max said.

Finley held her unused cup up for David to make the switch. She tasted her sister's coffee, which was still hot, and rich, and signaled for the waiter to bring Whitt some tea.

"In the meantime, you should get some water down you. You need to stave off a headache or you will be out for the rest of the day," Finley added. "And I know you don't want that."

Whitt gave her a side-eye under the brim of her hat. She began to add sugar to the cup of tea that the waiter had put in front of her. "A hit of sugar, and I'll be just fine."

"Can I get you some toast? Or something cool, like some fruit?" Logan asked with concern.

"No, I'll be fit as a fiddle in just a bit," Whitt muttered, pulling the hat further down.

"Whitt, if nothing else, you need to get out of the sun. Switch places with me so you can find a piece of shade." Finley stood to relinquish the shade provided by a small ironwood tree to her sister.

She put her bag on the seat between David and Logan, passed Whitt her fan, and turned toward the food. "Cool yourself down before you try to eat. But you'll need to put something in your stomach before we head out."

Max followed Finley over to the buffet. "Does she get heat-stroke easily?" he asked.

"No, she's pretty hearty. I think all that champagne yesterday may have been a contributing factor." Finley grinned as she picked up a plate. "I think she may have had double the amount that I had."

When Finley scanned the room, she saw Sandra and Elise each sitting alone at tables for two. Elise was pouring what looked like water into a large thermos. Into it, she dropped several lime slices. She carefully screwed the top on the bottle and put it in her straw bag. She nodded at Finley from a distance.

Finley elected to have an Indian breakfast, *kachori*, a puffy, fried pastry stuffed with potatoes, chutney, and a side of dal. She also put an *aloo paratha* and a mix of pickles and sweet chutney on her plate. She knew the paratha would probably sit heavy in her stomach later in the morning, but the smell of it was too tantalizing to pass up. She threw on a piece of papaya to make the mound look healthier.

Max smiled at the admixture of foods on her plate as he set down his bowl of fruit and another small plate with scrambled eggs and bacon. "You're an adventurous soul."

"Not really. This, or *dosa*, is what I have most mornings at the site. It fills you up," she laughed. "The cheat is the paratha, which I have real problems walking past."

"Mind if I try some?" Logan asked, his hand already in her plate, tearing off a piece of the paratha.

"Help yourself. If I eat all of this, I'll roll out of here." She leaned over to dollop some chutney on the piece of bread he had pulled off.

"What do you think?" She watched as Logan rolled the bread around the sweet chutney and popped it in his mouth. He closed his eyes to savor the mix of sweet and savory before sighing deeply.

"This is good. Really good," Logan finally said.

Max observed the brief exchange between Logan and Finley from across the table. The familiarity between the two of them rankled him. He couldn't put his finger on what bothered him about it, besides the comfort that existed between the two. She said they were friends, but how close were they really?

"The plan, according to Sandra, is that we're all going meet in the front lobby after breakfast and then head off sightseeing." Logan wiped a speck of chutney off his chin. "I took the restaurant up on the offer to pack us a hamper, so we didn't have to find a place for lunch."

"Who's coming on the tour?" Whitt asked. She had regained a bit of color and was spreading the slice of toast that David had passed across the table for her with butter and marmalade. "And now, may I please have some coffee?"

Finley drained her cup and poured more coffee before passing it to her sister. "You want something else to eat? I'll get it for you," Finley offered.

"I'll go with you. I don't know exactly what I want." Whitt got up and headed to the buffet. Finley followed close behind.

"You and Max okay?" Whitt reached for a roll and some jam.

"Yeah. Why do you ask?" Finley frowned slightly, looking over her shoulder to catch a glimpse of Max's profile. His strong jaw, the slight pout of his mouth. "Did he look upset?"

"Just a look I caught on his face." Whitt grabbed an apple, which Finley quickly took from her hand with a shake of her head.

"You and green apples don't get along. Don't push your luck." Finley added a few pieces of papaya and melon to her plate before turning to head back to the table. "Did you see what caused his reaction?"

"You and Logan," Whitt replied. "You weren't doing anything wrong. It was just the way Max looked at the two of you. I think he's jealous."

"Jealous? Of what?" Finley stopped midstep. "We are friends. Period."

"I know, but that may not be how Max sees it." Whitt headed off to the table, stopping to ask the waiter for more coffee along the way.

When Finley approached the table, she stood near Max and offered him some of her fruit. He declined, but Finley remained standing beside him while she ate a few bites of the papaya. He instinctively draped his arm around her legs and pulled her closer.

"What time are we meeting out front?" Finley asked Logan.

"At nine. So, we have a few more minutes," he replied.

"Time for another cup of coffee." Finley slipped into her seat and reached for the coffee pot.

"I'll pour," Logan offered, filling Finley's cup before topping his off. Finley looked across David in time to see Max's jaw flex. *He is jealous. This is absurd. What will it take for him to believe that we are just friends?*

The quick trip to Jal Mahal started in crowded cityscape before opening suddenly to mountainous countryside. The sandstone palace itself was a spectacular sight, an architectural masterpiece that used the lake in which it sat and the hills surrounding it to complement its glory. A center garden terrace anchored the rectangular building, which sported four octagonal towers, each capped with an elegantly carved cupola. When the lake was high, small boats carried tourists out to circle the majestic castle.

The car with the Four Musketeers pulled into a clearing on the shore of the lake, and Darsh directed them to the dock, where other guests from the Rambaugh stood. Hema and her parents, as well as the couple from the UAE, took shelter from the morning sun under a large tree. Finley was glad to see that each of the boats was outfitted with a large, colorful umbrella.

The boat operators had almost finished loading the various groups into the vessels when Logan, Sandra, and Elise pulled up.

"Don't leave us! Sorry we're late." Logan opened the door for Elise and gave her his arm, while Vik helped Sandra. "Sandra misplaced her bracelet, and it took her a while to find it."

The threesome was quickly loaded onto a boat, and the small flotilla of brightly colored vessels cast off. The sun was arcing in the sky, reflecting off the plate glass surface of the water. The stillness of the water, even with the moving boats, made it seem as if they were skimming on its surface rather than cutting through it.

Finley had left the bulk of her equipment in the car with Darsh, taking only the most compact of her cameras with her in her backpack. She was still learning how to photograph water. She took her time playing with the settings and testing the effect on the images. Max watched her as she worked, a half smile playing on his lips.

After a while, she put away the camera and leaned into Max. She took his hand in hers and gently kissed it. She looked over at her sister, who was seeking what little shade the umbrella provided as she leaned on David's shoulder, his arm holding her tightly. *Life is good. If only it can stay this way.*

Finley cast her eyes back to shore and saw Ravi and another man standing near the dock. She scanned the parking area for a car in which Devya might be sitting but saw none. The bearded man, who was taller and larger than Ravi, was gesturing wildly and at one point seemed to grab Ravi by the shirtfront. Ravi appeared to be trying to calm the man down but with little result. In time, the man walked off, turning once to shout something at Ravi before getting into a truck and driving off. After the man left, Ravi walked out of view. Shortly after, a gray sedan pulled out and blended into traffic.

"What are you looking at so intently?" Max asked.

"I thought I saw Ravi."

"Are he and Devya trying to get a boat to make the tour?"

"Doesn't appear so. I didn't see Devya," Finley said. "He was talking to a man, and then they both drove off. Strange."

"Probably nothing. May not even have been Ravi."

"You may be right. And even if it were, what of it? It's just so relaxing out here. Even in the heat!"

By the time all the groups had come back to shore, the drivers had lined up, ready to take them to Jaigarh Fort, up in the hills.

The line of cars wound their way up the mountain, heading to the fortification that housed the largest cannon in the world. From this vantage, tourists got an eagle's view of the Amber Fort and the hills surrounding it. Standing on the parapet, it became clear why the fort's location in the narrow mountain pass gave it a strategic advantage.

Lunch after the tour of the fort was a sumptuous feast of grilled meats and vegetables, various flatbreads, chutneys, and pickles. Vik and the other drivers spread beautiful old rugs on the ground in a shaded area midway down the mountain. From there, the group could see the water and the far hills as well as both the Amber Fort and Jal Mahal.

Logan had apparently broken from his bejeweled twosome at some point during the last tour and joined Hema and her parents for lunch. His laughter could be heard several rugs away. Finley smiled at the sound of it. He was a man who surely enjoyed life and wasn't afraid to show it. *I am so lucky to have him as a friend. He is a genuinely sweet man.*

When the hampers and rugs had been packed away, and the monkeys appeased with leftover fruit and scraps of bread, the Rambaugh caravan set off for the nearby Amber Fort. While Finley and Max opted to walk up the steep, walled path that led from the water to the palace, Whitt, David, and the others decided to take the festooned elephants up the stone trail. After leaving Hema with her parents, Logan had hopped into a travel basket with Ravi, who had appeared from nowhere.

The elephants were no more than halfway up the severe incline when several of the mahouts called out. Max and Finley turned to see two of the mahouts guide their elephants over to a third animal. The mahout for the third elephant had deftly climbed down the magnificent beast, who stood patiently waiting. After a time, there was considerable shouting and waving of hands among the mahouts and the small crowd of shopkeepers and others that had gathered to observe. From the scrum of people crowding around the elephant, Logan and Ravi emerged, shaking their heads.

"Well, I guess we're walking," Logan remarked. The travel basket they had been in sat pushed to the side, its elephant and mahout apparently sidelined. The other elephants and their passengers trudged slowly up the hill.

"What gives? You get scared of the height?" Finley waited for Logan and then walked in step beside him.

"Apparently the strap under the beast broke." Ravi appeared agitated by the experience. He kept looking back at the broken travel basket and the elephant, who seemed to be enjoying the break. "The handler said it was cut. He said he had checked all the rigging when he came out this morning and it was fine."

"Why would anyone cut the girth?" Max asked. He had settled himself at Finley's other side.

"Beats me," Logan said. "But he was pretty insistent. In any case, I gave him the full fare and a big tip, since he's out of commission for the day, at least."

"Did you have fun for the short time that you were on?" Finley asked.

"As always. I like traveling by elephant," Logan replied. "I had occasion to do some trekking by elephant in Thailand and enjoyed it."

He looked past Finley to engage Max. "You didn't want a ride?"

Max glanced at him briefly before fixing his stare ahead. "No, I rather enjoy walking."

Finley slowed her pace and took his hand as they continued up the rest of the winding cobbles.

The fort, which had also served as a luxurious palace, was a fine example of Mughal architecture, with its four levels and multiple, interconnected red sandstone and marble buildings. In fact, the guide leading the Rambaugh group around the labyrinth of stone walkways and arches said that Amber and Jaigarh Forts were considered one complex, given the subterranean passageways that connected them.

It was easy to get lost in the myriad rooms and outbuildings of the palace. The different levels of the structure each had similar features, including a courtyard. While taking pictures in the Hall of Mirrors, built in the sixteenth century using technology adopted from the Turks, who'd introduced it some eight hundred years before, Finley became separated from the others.

She wandered to the section marked as the royal bedchambers. As the guide had said, she found a maze of rooms, all with stairs leading to a large chamber. Purportedly, the Raja had twelve wives, and while there were twelve flights of stairs, the queens were not allowed to go upstairs. Only the Raja could come down. *Slightly misogynistic but probably a good distribution of the burden of looking after a self-absorbed husband.*

At the end of the passageway connecting the rooms, Finley found a large turret room that looked out onto the interior cascades built to create natural air-conditioning for the palace. The tower gave her a view of the lovely gardens and pools below as well as the hillside vantage of Jaigarh Fort and the Great Wall–like parapet that ran between the two. She was so absorbed in capturing pictures of both tableaus that she didn't hear Logan enter the room.

He stood watching her work, trying to follow with his eye what she was seeing through the lens.

"So, there you are. I was wondering where you had gotten to," he commented.

Finley smiled. "I got lost, so I took advantage of it to grab some pictures."

"Do you know where the others are?" Logan moved alongside her to look through the open arches of the turret.

"Nope." Finley had gone back to taking photos. "We'll find them, I'm sure."

It took the two a bit of twisting and turning before they got their bearings and made their way to the large center courtyard that housed the museum. Hema and her parents were already sitting on the ledge in front of the museum shop. Logan and Finley took a seat beside them. It was there that Max found them, sitting side by side, looking at shots on Finley's camera.

"Where'd you get to?" Max tried to make his voice sound light, but Finley picked up on the tension.

"I got lost and ran into Logan." Finley planted a kiss on Max's cheek. "We found our way back here, and I was just showing him some shots I got. Want to see?"

"Maybe later." Max fixed on her face, his jaw flexing. "Where are Whitt and David?"

"In the shop, of course! They got back a couple of minutes ago and went shopping. It's anybody's guess what she'll find in there." Finley leaned her head on his shoulder. "Did you have a good time wandering?"

"Once I stopped looking for you," Max said tightly.

"I'm sorry. I tried to find you. I sent you a text." Finley looked up at him, but he was staring at a fixed point in front of him. "Then I got caught up taking pictures."

Max was silent. Finley didn't know what else to say. She returned her head to his shoulder and listened to his breathing. She knew he was angry, but she didn't know why. So, she waited, like she always did, until things became clearer.

"Y'all ready?" Whitt broke into the moment.

"What did you get?" Finley asked, looking into the bags that her sister held out.

"Just a few things for Mama and Daddy. And, of course, Charlie and the folks in the office."

"Yeah, just a few things." David laughed at the mound of bags in front of them. "Thank goodness we aren't making any other stops before we get back to the hotel."

6

THE DRIVEWAY IN FRONT OF the hotel had no fewer than five police cars parked side by side. As the touring procession came to a halt, the turbaned doorman greeted each guest and asked that they wait in the lobby before proceeding to their rooms.

"I wonder what this is about," Whitt said. "I would like a little rest before dinner and then a little something cool to drink—preferably alcoholic."

"Ditto on that." Finley took a seat on one of the tasseled divans and patted the place beside her to signal Max to join her. He had been virtually mute during the trip back to the hotel. She still wasn't sure what she had done, if anything, to prompt his steeliness. What she did know was that a "conversation" was coming, and those rarely ended well.

Within ten minutes, Patel, the resident manager, and a severe-looking, uniformed gentleman addressed the group. Logan had resumed his role as Sandra and Elise's escort. Hema sat with her parents. Ravi stood, leaning against the wall, and the Emirati couple took seats nearby.

"We apologize for the inconvenience, but, as you may be aware, one of our staff, a young houseboy, died last night. We had initially thought that it was a snakebite." Patel shifted his weight from foot to foot, looking periodically at the slight officer beside him before continuing. "However, the police now have reason to believe that he took, or was given, a very strong sedative, to which he was allergic."

The assembled group gasped at the revelation and began to talk among themselves. Patel raised his voice to be heard above the din.

"Inspector Das is trying to determine both the nature and the source of the sedative that was found in the boy's system. As such, he has asked to search each of our guests' rooms." He paused, unsure what else to say. "Again, we apologize for the inconvenience and hope that the police will have your full cooperation."

The uniformed officer stepped forward and, in a voice that made clear who was in charge, began to issue instructions. He was bantamweight in build but commanded a presence that brooked no silliness or disobedience. Each guest or family was assigned an officer who would follow them to their rooms, where an inspection would be conducted. That they would cooperate fully was understood.

A single policeman was assigned to the suite shared by Whitt, David, Finley, and Max. The officer asked for all medications to be laid out on the desk in each room. He then took pictures of the labels. He inquired about contact with Ajai, the houseboy, and the last time that he was seen. Finley had to think about this last question. He had been an affable boy, eager to practice his English and willing to work hard for a tip. After a few more perfunctory questions, the policeman left.

"That was strange." Whitt stuck her head inside the still-open door to Finley and Max's room. "I'm trying to figure out how that sort of inspection is going to yield much of anything."

David followed her partway into the room. "I agree, but it isn't our problem. And I, for one, want a nap before we get cleaned up for dinner."

"Sounds good to me." Finley looked at Max for confirmation. He shrugged in response. "Are we grazing again or sitting down for a proper dinner?"

"If you don't mind, can we head into the restaurant tonight?" David smiled. "You guessed it—I'm hungry!"

Whitt kissed his cheek. "Of course, you are. Shall we meet at seven thirty in the dining room? I'll make us a reservation. Tootles!"

Whitt let David pass before closing the door. Finley stood awkwardly in the sitting room, looking at Max as he fiddled with something on his phone. She knew the "conversation" was soon to start but didn't know whether she or he was to initiate. If she was supposed to take the first step, she had no idea what she would say. While she stood pondering, Max took the lead.

"So, you want to tell me what's going on with you and Logan?" Max looked at her from across the room.

"Nothing. He's a friend. I want to be sure that he's having a good time. Whether you like it or not, he's our guest."

Max started to respond but then checked himself. His face flushed, and he tried to slow his breathing. "Are you telling me that the events yesterday, this morning, and this afternoon had no meaning whatsoever?" Max's voice was measured. His eyes pierced through her with an intensity she had never experienced. *He is beyond angry, but I still don't know what I did.*

"Max, I can see that you are upset, but I can't address what I don't know about or understand," Finley spoke softly. "Please help me understand. I don't know what events you're talking about."

"The kiss yesterday, feeding him this morning, and running off with him this afternoon." Max crossed the room and stood in front of Finley. His eyes narrowed and locked with hers.

"What?" Finley's mouth dropped open. *Where is he getting this? He's accusing me of betraying him. I would never.*

She swallowed hard to control the tears. "I would never betray you. I was thanking him yesterday for being my friend. And I didn't run off with him this afternoon; I got lost and we ended up in the same section of the fort."

"And I'm supposed to believe that?" Max shook his head and sat down hard in a sitting room chair. He gave an incredulous half laugh.

Finley sat down on the sofa across from him, hoping to defuse what had become one of the worst arguments she had ever had with Max in the three years they had been together. Her chest tightened. She was finding it hard to breath. A single tear slipped down her cheek. She hurriedly brushed it away.

"You can believe what you want. If you can't trust me, take me at my word, then what does that say about our relationship?"

Her voice was quiet. Her pace had slowed as if the world were moving in slow motion. Her gaze never left his face. His beautiful face that was now twisted into an angry scowl she neither liked nor understood. It was the lack of understanding, the mired confusion, that pained her most.

"That I don't like it when you hang around other men."

"So, I can't have men friends? Should I be careful when I'm around David, too? You never know."

"Don't be absurd. Of course, you can be with David."

"So, it's just men that you think I've been in a relationship with?" The words flew from her mouth before she could stop them. She wasn't sure anymore that she wanted to stop them.

He has got to be kidding. He wants to dictate my life—and without making any sort of commitment to me. Three years. Three years, I will never get back. He has a lot of nerve. He wants to stake a claim without paying the deposit.

"You're telling me you weren't in a relationship with Logan?"

"No! Logan and I were never in a relationship. We're friends and always have been."

"You're telling me you've never kissed him?"

"Yes, I've kissed him but—"

"Have you—"

"Don't go there, Max. Don't erode every ounce of trust we have by asking for my personal history unless you're willing to give me yours." Finley bit out the words, the hurt and humiliation embedded in every syllable. The tears flowed freely now, and she didn't try to stem them. "I know you've had other lovers, and I have never asked about them because I trust you."

Max was silent, thinking, his jaw tense. He rose from the chair and stood, unmoving, in front of it. He faced her but stared fixedly at some unknown object on the floor. His chest rose and fell as he took in heavy breaths of air, his jaw flexing all the while.

She spoke in a raspy whisper, fighting to keep the tears from drowning out her words. "I've put my life on hold to be with you. Logan was there, but I chose you. And yet, whatever I do, it never seems to be enough. Maybe the reality is that I'm not enough for you."

Max paused, his stare still fixed, before walking over to the night table and picking up his watch and his phone. He checked his pocket for his wallet. When he got to the door, he stopped. "I think it's best if I claim the couch tonight." The door clicked shut behind him.

Finley sat on the sofa and let the tears and sobs she had fought valiantly to hold back wash over her. She was numb. She hoped no one had heard the exchange. She laughed to herself that, amid the tsunami hitting her now, she still cared what others might think, whether she had inconvenienced them in some way.

She didn't know how long she had sat there, in the same place, not moving for fear her heart and the rest of her might shatter if she dared move. The sun had gone down. She suspected she needed to get ready for dinner. She wondered where Max had gone. Part of her wanted to go after him, to somehow make it right, but she knew it might never be right again.

She ran herself a deep bath and poured in bath salts, as if those might ease the pain in her chest. She went through the motions of choosing the right dress for this evening, something with color so the vacuous look in her eyes wasn't so noticeable. She carefully applied her makeup, like a robot programmed to complete all assigned tasks, regardless of the circumstances.

When she reached the dining room, Whitt and David were already seated. Whitt was sipping on a glass of champagne, while the waiter poured David a beer.

"I waited to see what you're having before I ordered a bottle," Whitt said. "Do you want champagne or something else?"

"Champagne is fine." Finley searched to find a neutral voice that would betray nothing.

"Where's Max? Is he not coming to dinner?" Whitt asked casually.

"I don't think he'll make dinner tonight," Finley said quietly. "It will just be the three of us."

David took a sip of his beer and peered at Whitt over his glass. Whitt shrugged in reply.

"Did you get some good shots today?" David looked to Whitt to be sure that this was a safe topic of conversation.

Finley picked up the thread. "I got quite a few frames that may turn out to be interesting. There was a tower near the royal bedchambers that had a great view of the cascades and Jaigarh. I wonder whether that was where you were sent as a queen if you misbehaved."

"Better than to the Tower of London," Whitt quipped. She wished that she and Finley were sharing a room tonight so that she could get at what was going on with her and Max. She missed their sister-to-sister, late-night talks. David had given her some idea about Max being in a weird place, but he didn't know anything else. Maybe she could get David to ferret out more.

"It looks like Logan and Hema may be hitting it off." David had directed their attention to a table across the room. "He also joined her and her parents for lunch today."

"He deserves someone special."

Finley was in a strangely wistful mood. The argument with Max had unsettled her, but it had also increased her resolve to redefine what happiness meant for her. Perhaps she had been too wrapped up in being what Max wanted that she had forgotten about what she wanted. *You just got thrown. Hard. Don't waste your time trying to figure out why it happened. Just accept that it did. Lick your wounds and move on.*

"You like Logan, don't you?" David had turned his attention back to Finley. His voice had softened with the question.

"I do. He's a very dear friend and a really good man," Finley said quietly. "He helped me get through a rough time. He could have decided I wasn't worth the effort, but he didn't. And for that, I'll always treasure his kindness."

David was silent for a moment. "Have you explained that to Max?"

Finley drew in a breath and held it, unsure how to respond. Max and Logan in the same sentence seemed to cause nothing but problems. She thought she had explained it, but clearly not.

"I've tried, but I guess I didn't do too good of a job." Finley looked down at her fish. She had barely taken a bite. She wasn't hungry, but it seemed pointless to waste it. She took another bite, chewed, and swallowed. *One foot in front of the other. If you can just get through the next couple of days, you can figure out the rest. Just get through the next few days.*

She realized she had missed a good part of the conversation with her self-talk. Whitt was observing her over the rim of her champagne flute. David was pretending to concentrate on his curry.

"Okay, what did I miss? I know I was in my own little world. Sorry," she said.

"Nothing. I was just saying that we were thinking of heading to Agra tomorrow, if you want to go."

Whitt still eyed Finley. Something was going on. She didn't know what, but she wasn't sure she liked it. Finley was trying too hard, a sure sign that she was protecting herself—or someone else. *If he hurts her again, I'll kill him myself. She deserves better than this.*

"Are we even allowed to go outside Jaipur?" Finley asked. "We don't know what Inspector Das found in the search and what follow-up questions he might have."

"Do you think the kid was murdered?" Whitt asked, her eyes wide.

"I'm not sure. But how did he get the sedative in him? It's unlikely that he took it on purpose. He was a kid."

"It had to be an accident, then," David said. "Why would anyone purposely hurt a kid?"

"I don't know. But, as far as I know, the police haven't said we have to stay in Jaipur, so we are going to Agra." Whitt was defiant in her statement, but she looked at David for confirmation all the same.

"Then go ahead and take the car. I need to cull the pictures I have, and then I may head over to Nahagarh. But I can take a taxi from here. They say the view of the city from there is worth seeing." Finley smiled at her sister. *I hope she doesn't get herself arrested for defying a police order. I heard the Indian jails are the stuff of legend.*

Finley left David and Whitt haggling over which dessert to have. In the end, she knew they would end up with two. Whitt would then take a taste of each before passing them to David to finish. She loved watching their play fights, but tonight she was spent. She didn't have the heart or the energy to pretend anymore. She headed back to her room, ready to face whatever came next. As much as she dreaded finding Max in the room, she dreaded returning to an empty room even more.

She switched on the light and looked for some indication that he had been there. There was none. After attempting to read, she got up and changed into her night clothes. There was no point in denying it. She missed him. The thought of being without him, perhaps forever, triggered the tears. She let them fall until she drifted off to sleep, exhausted.

David found Max in the bar, where he had apparently been all evening. He sat with an empty wine glass in front of him while he nursed a whiskey. He didn't look inebriated, but Max himself had suggested when they were in Morocco that he was a highly functional drunk. David wondered whether a run would help him get this bout of desperation out of his system. From the looks of it, he doubted it.

"Come to give me grief or join me in it?" Max looked up, with a crooked smile, to greet his friend.

"Neither. Just to find out what's going on," David said, signaling the waiter for a beer. This may be a long night. He wanted to help, and listening might be the best way. Something was eating at Max, and it had been twisting his innards for a long time. He had noticed Max's funk since they arrived in Delhi, but Max always seemed to be able to pull himself out before he went into a complete tailspin. This time was clearly different.

"You've seen Finley, I take it?"

"She was at dinner."

"So, she went anyway?"

"Does that surprise you?" David wondered why that bothered Max. Finley was trying her best not to be the downer at the party, as far as David could see.

"Yes and no. It just gets complicated," Max laughed, then took a sip of his drink. He winced as it burned his throat.

"Then why don't you explain it to me so I can understand. I've got all night." David raised his beer.

Max sat silent for a couple of minutes, his eyes half-hooded by drink and saddened by doubt. "Do you think she ever loved me?" He set his glass down and lowered his head into his hands.

"I don't think she has ever loved anyone but you. Why do you think she doesn't?"

"Are you blind, too? Or am I the only one seeing something wrong with her hanging on Logan at every chance?"

"He's her friend. Someone who helped her when she needed it. She wants him to have a good time," David said. "I don't think it's any more than that. Sounds like Logan accepts that he lost to the better man and he's okay with being her friend."

"And you truly believe that?" Max raised his head and gave David a piercing look.

"I do." David paused. "From what I've heard, she went through hell trying to get over you and decided she couldn't."

"And so, she flirts with an old boyfriend in front of my face? Interesting."

"As far as I can see, she hasn't been flirting. Having fun with a friend, but not flirting. I think the things she has done with Logan are the same things she would do with any friend. Mooney or Charlie, even."

"So, this is all my imagination?" Max sat looking at David, scanning his face with purpose. David wasn't sure what he was looking for. Some flaw in his logic or evidence of dissembling. What he did know was that something was driving the jealousy, something that had nothing to do with Finley.

"Not your imagination, but your perception," David said. "Look, Max, you're going to feel what you feel and who am I to say that you shouldn't be suspicious. But what I will say is that maybe there is another way to look at it, and that's the way she sees it. Just a thought."

FINLEY THOUGHT SHE HAD HEARD Max at some point during the night, the soft purr of his breathing, but when she got up the next morning, he wasn't there. Drops of water on the counter in the bathroom confirmed that she hadn't been dreaming. As did the folded-up blanket and sheets left on the end of the desk.

She showered and got dressed. She decided on room service for breakfast. She didn't feel like small talk this morning. Just coffee and fruit. And an *aloo paratha*. She wanted comfort food, even if it would make her lethargic later in the day. She wanted to be comforted now. If her sister hadn't left for Agra already, she might have given in and shared with her the pain that sat heavy on her heart.

But she had heard Whitt and David in the hall before dawn this morning. She hadn't slept well, waking in fits and starts before drifting back into another bout of broken sleep. She might take a nap later in the day. She was glad reviewing the frames didn't take much concentration.

She prayed that she could just coast through the next few days, pretending all was okay, until she got back to Delhi and then on to

Jharkhand. She paused midway through the sequence. She didn't have a "home" in Delhi anymore, she realized.

She and Max might be able to fake it until Whitt and David left, and then she would have to find herself another place to live. Or maybe she would just pack her things and take them back to Jharkhand with her. Once her project was finished, she could ask Dan for another assignment far, far away from here.

The thought of being upended, untethered, yet again unleashed another flood of tears. *Finley, you need to get a grip. You cannot start acting crazy like you did last time you two broke up. Mama will not put up with another bout of breakdown.*

She laughed out loud as she recalled Mama watching her cut her hair off, like a mad Medusa, when she first got back from Morocco. The woman had gone apoplectic at the sight of Finley's long tresses gathered up in a plastic bag for the wigmaker. Only Daddy had been able to calm her down. The poor man had had two women crying hysterically for reasons he could not discern. He had simply sat between the two, wiping their tears, until they collected themselves, harrumphed, and walked off in different directions without a word.

Finley sat on the sofa in the sitting room, her cameras laid out in front of her. She had just finished scrolling through the frames on the first camera when she noticed something on the entryway table moving in the fan breeze. She removed the note that was stuck under a vase of flowers and recognized Max's elegant writing.

"Gone for a run" had been scratched through and "Working" had replaced it. Finley turned the note over, looking for more and, seeing none, began to add importance to the single word. *Well, at least he hasn't packed up and left. That he's working is a good sign. Maybe it will redirect his anger.*

She poured herself another cup of coffee, note in hand. *This is sick. Trying to read meaning into a single word. You still don't know what you did, besides have fun with a friend, and you're worried about whether he's still angry and how he's doing. You need to stop walking on eggshells around Max. It isn't healthy, and you know it. He's the one with the problem, not you.*

Finley went to the house phone in the room and asked for a car to take her to Nahargarh Fort. It was still early morning. She could cull her pictures later. Right now, she needed to get out of the room, get some air. She pulled her backpack from the closet and packed it with a folding tripod, her travel pack of filters, and a couple of extra lenses. She scanned the equipment on the table, debating over which of her cameras to take. Having decided on the lightest, she shoved the others into the safe and locked it. She considered leaving a note for Max and opted against it.

When she arrived at Nahargarh, she hired a guide to show her around the mammoth structure. Part fort, part palace, and part hunting lodge, Nahargarh commanded the hilltop with a breathtaking view of the city of Jaipur and the surrounding hills. The stunning arched parapets that encircled the palace afforded a window onto the sprawling pink and white city below. With its sister forts, Jaigarh and Amber, Nahargarh had provided a solid defense perimeter for the city.

After almost two hours of wandering the grounds, Finley thanked her guide for the tour and began retracing her steps so that she could take the time she needed to get the best shots of the panoramic tableau the fort provided. She settled into a rhythm of scouting the best angle, finding the best lens and filter, and taking test shots. She had repeated it at least six times before she heard her name. She turned to find Logan, Sandra, and Elise walking toward her.

"Where did you come from?" Sandra asked, smiling. "We didn't see you at breakfast and figured you and the boyfriend wanted a little quiet time."

"Max is working, so I decided to come up and get some photos of the city," Finley said. She wasn't lying, just stretching the truth a bit. "The views from here are phenomenal."

"They are indeed. Did you just get here?" Elise asked. She took a drink from her thermos and closed the top. Finley caught a metallic smell with a hint of lime. Definitely not just water. "It's so hot up here. We're going to head down the hill and do a bit of shopping at the arcades near the Hawa Mahal. Want to come?"

"No, I think I'll stick around here. I just finished a tour and want to get some shots of the scenery," Finley replied. She didn't have to tell them that she needed some time to herself, some time to focus on something other than the ache in her chest. Concentrated work might help. "Have fun, though."

Logan moved to stand beside Finley.

"You know, if you ladies don't mind, I think I'll hang out here a little longer. I haven't had a chance to catch up with Finley since we got here, with all the touring. I'll just grab the chance now," Logan said. "You can take the car. If Finley doesn't have a driver, we can have the hotel send one."

Finley got ready to protest. All she needed, with Max in a mood, was to have him see the two of them together. *But you aren't doing anything wrong, so why should it matter? Stop jumping through hoops for Max. Logan's right. Except for group conversations, you've had little time to talk to him. Take the time now.*

Sandra and Elise shrugged. "If you are sure you won't need the car, we'll take you up on it."

When Elise and Sandra headed for the exit and their shopping trip, Finley started rechecking her shots. She needed to get some photos from the parapets that surrounded the expansive grounds.

"Where are the others?" Finley asked, having climbed the stone lookouts to get her shots. "Did any of them come touring with you?"

"Hema and her parents were here, and Ravi finally got Devya out."

"That was probably a monumental task." Finley smiled. "That's not very nice of me. This may just not be her thing, going to see old castles and fortresses. Maybe if he took her shopping."

"I think he tried that. She just isn't happy here."

65

"Well, we'll be heading back to Delhi soon."

Logan watched her work, at one point leaning over a restraining wall to get an unobstructed view of the city below. He admired her focus, her dedication to getting better at her craft. After a time, he started to say something but stopped. Finley looked up from her camera to see what was wrong. He still hesitated, seemingly unsure what to say next, very much unlike his usual self-assured bearing.

"Okay, Logan, out with it!"

"This—being with me—won't get you in trouble with Max, will it?" Logan finally asked. "He can get pretty testy when I'm around. I guess if I had a woman as pretty as you for a girlfriend, I would protect my territory, too."

Finley laughed and raised her camera again. "You do. I saw you at dinner with Hema. And Max will just have to deal with the fact that we're friends."

"So, you saw us. We were trying to be discreet," Logan said. "Kind of hard when there are only so many restaurants on the grounds."

"I guess so, but you could have taken her someplace off the grounds. The hotel could have arranged it."

"Her parents are a little wary of me. Cultural differences, age differences. They're progressive, but it only goes so far."

"Well, I can vouch for your integrity and fine moral standing," Finley joked.

"I wish you would." Logan grew serious. "I kind of like her. Actually, I'm really quite taken with her, truth be told."

Finley stopped her shooting and looked at her friend. He was looking over the battlements, out toward the city. The haze that normally hung over the desert city had lifted so that the view of both the city and the hills was clear.

"This is serious. You haven't said you liked a woman like this almost since I met you."

"That's because you keep getting in the way." Logan play punched her. "You almost finished? It's lunchtime. Let's go grab something to eat. They have a teahouse on the grounds."

Finley and Logan found a seat near the front of the teahouse where they could catch the breeze and take in the view. There were several other tourists having tea, but none from the Rambaugh. Finley enjoyed being quasi-anonymous. She suspected that Logan liked it, too. In New York, it was impossible for him to go into a restaurant without at least two or three people coming up to shake his hand. She realized that she missed talking to him, spending time with him, like they did in New York.

"So, fill me in on you and Hema," Finley probed, after they had placed their order for an assortment of *pakoras* for Finley and a vegetarian *thali* for Logan. When their lime sodas came, they both drank thirstily.

"Not much to fill in, really. I like her. She's got a wicked sense of humor, likes travel and art, a lot of the things that I like. And I think she may like me. At least, she hasn't stopped taking my texts."

"How can she not like you? You are the biggest catch in all of New York. Probably in the world. The Millionaire Matchmaker would have a field day with you!" Finley remembered the looks she used to get when the two of them were together in the city. The women who would fall over themselves to get close to him, to have him acknowledge their existence. Women who wanted to scratch her eyes out when he focused his attention solely on her, giving them little notice.

"We'll see. Have you and Max been able to get away and have a little fun? I heard Whitt and David headed to the Taj Mahal." Logan signaled the waiter for another round of lime sodas while he pulled out his phone. He grew pensive looking at the screen. "I'm going to have to figure out how to see that before I go. Maybe a helicopter flight up from Delhi. Do you think Hema's parents will allow that?"

"Oh, the things you can do with money." Finley shook her head.

"Are there things you would do if you were rolling in dough?" Logan rested his chin in his palm. "Dream away, my sweet!"

"They would probably all be philanthropic. There isn't much I want for myself. I'm doing what I like. So, life is good."

"You are such a simple creature," Logan laughed. "And I mean that only in the best way. But you really are content."

"Folks back home would probably howl if they heard that! I'm considered high-maintenance. Not as HM as Whitt or Mama, but still very HM, all the same."

"It's all relative," Logan said with a smile. "But you didn't answer my question about you and Max. Are you avoiding it?"

"It's complicated." Finley stared at her tea. Now would not be the best time or place for the tears to start again. She could feel them welling up. She swallowed hard to regain control. Her jaw worked back and forth as she tried to slow her breathing.

"Finley." Logan touched her arm. "Talk to me."

Finley sat, silent. The tears came one at a time. For that, she was glad. She reached in her backpack and pulled out a Kleenex.

Logan's voice was soft. He kept his hand on her arm and tried to catch a look at her face from under the mass of hair that had escaped her hairclip.

"Did you and Max argue, sweetie?" Logan paused. "Over me?"

Finley remained silent. Whatever she said wouldn't make sense, or at least, she couldn't make sense of it. The thought of the situation with Max tired her. She didn't want to talk about it anymore.

"Can we change the subject?" Her eyes implored him to agree.

"Sure, kid." Logan removed his hand and sat back, watching her. After a moment or two he asked, "You seem to be good at solving puzzles. What do you think happened to Ajai, the houseboy at the hotel?"

Logan was trying to distract her and was doing a good job of it. She had been thinking about the boy's death in between bouts of tears and sleeplessness. The police hadn't said any more about who had been the source of the sedative. They also hadn't carted anyone off for questioning or subjected anyone to a second round of interrogation. For all intents and purposes, the police acted like the investigation was closed.

"I don't know. Patel said the boy had an allergic reaction. Maybe he found something in one of the rooms and took it as an experiment or drank something from one of the trays that he shouldn't have."

"That's an interesting supposition. I always wonder whether the waitstaff or cleaning staff sample the food or drinks that guests only half finish. Maybe he took a sip out of one of the glasses that someone had used to mix a sleeping powder."

"But if that were the case, then they would have matched someone at the Rambaugh as the source of the sedative, and that would have been the end of the story."

"So, you're saying, because they haven't said they could match it, they can't close it as an accident. Which means that it came from outside the hotel and anyone could have brought it in for any reason."

"You got it. And that's scary."

"Yeah, it is," Logan said quietly. "On that happy note, we probably should head back."

When they were in the car heading back to the Rambaugh, Logan shifted in his seat to look directly at Finley. He hesitated to pick at the scab that was Max, but he needed to clear the air. "I know you don't want to talk about it, but I do. So, I'll do the talking." He drew a long breath. "Finley, I'm so sorry that I, this trip, and all of this has caused problems with you and Max. Sometimes I don't think about how I complicate people's lives. I never meant to upend things for you. I simply thought it would be fun to see you and Max in your natural environment. To get to know him better, since he's so much a part of your life." He sighed. "What can I do to make things right for you? I can see how you're hurting, and it pains me."

"Logan, Max and I have to work through this. You didn't cause this. Quite honestly, neither did I. We haven't done anything wrong, besides be friends. It's better that I learned this about him now. It'll work out, one way or the other." Finley put her hand in Logan's. They rode the rest of the trip in companionable silence.

Logan slid out and took Finley's arm when they got back to the hotel. They nodded to the doorman and headed through the lobby. When they got to the arcade, he paused.

"Look, I need to grab something from the shop. You okay getting back to your room?"

"Of course, silly. I came alone, so I think I know my way back to my room!" She turned and kissed him on the cheek. "Thanks for a delightful afternoon."

On the way to the room, she stopped to take some photos of the *charbagh*, or foursquare courtyard garden, from the bridge that connected the lobby to the rest of the hotel. She had admired the water-stone-landscaping composition, but there had often been gardeners interrupting the background when she had stopped for shots before. Today, the scene was picture perfect. After she got her shots, she resumed her walk to the room, half looking at the camera screen, half checking her direction. She didn't see Max until she was right up on him.

Her breath caught. She almost screamed from surprise but checked herself before it escaped.

"That didn't take long." He scanned her face with his eyes, assessing more than observing.

"What?" Finley hadn't any idea what he was talking about.

"You and Logan. Out on the town already!" His smirk was unnerving, almost sinister.

Finley stepped back and walked around him without responding. When she had gone some distance, she looked over her shoulder, not even trying to mask the look of disgust on her face. *How dare he! How fricking dare he!*

8

FINLEY DIDN'T CARE IF MAX caught her in the act. Nothing he could say was going to stop her from leaving. She'd had enough. Enough of the accusations. Enough of the innuendos. Enough of the on-again, off-again cycle of their relationship. She was out.

She laid all her clothes on the bed and then carefully folded and placed them in her duffle. She gathered her toiletries from the bathroom, slipped them into a Ziploc, and shoved them into her bag. She had already called the airlines and booked the 9:00 p.m. Air India flight to Delhi for that evening. She planned to sit in the coffee shop until the car arrived to take her to the airport.

She had packed away most of her camera equipment except for the lightweight camera she had used that day. The packing had taken her less time than she'd expected. She had over an hour before the car came, all of which she didn't want to spend sitting in a restaurant. Perhaps she'd take a few parting photos of the grounds before she left.

She stuck her head out of the door, looking to see if Max was lurking nearby. She didn't want to see Logan or the rest of the touring group either. She wanted to slip away and get to the airport. She would send explanatory texts from there. She had thought about a note to her sister, but she hadn't the slightest idea what to write—"I have gone off the deep end again" or "I have left him," when, in fact, he had left first.

Seeing no one on the veranda, she slipped out, locking the door behind her. She walked to the far end of the corridor and entered the green. Standing on the massive expanse of lawn, she turned back toward the hotel and began to click through several frames. She realized after a few frames that she hadn't switched out her fisheye for a standard lens, but she liked the perspective. She panned the hotel vista, taking in the entire back side of the building. These would offer an appropriate final view of the hotel's grandeur.

As she opened the door some minutes later, she saw a note on the floor. Whitt was back. So much for slipping away unseen.

"Don't know where you have gotten to but stop by my room when you get back! Love, Whitt."

Finley dropped her camera in her carry-on and shoved it under the desk. She checked her makeup in the mirror—no tear tracks—grabbed her key and headed next door.

"So, how was it?" Finley asked when her sister opened the door. She focused on keeping her voice cheerful. "Where's David?"

"He went to get a little something to tide him over until dinner. You know him. He's always hungry."

Finley then asked, "What did you think of Agra and the Taj?" Finley flopped down in one of the chairs in the sitting room and looked at her sister. Something was different. Whitt was trying to act nonchalant, but Finley could sense that her energy was bubbling over beneath the surface. She knew they hadn't had an argument or broken up because Whitt was animated, chatty even. *I can't figure it out. And I haven't the energy to try to guess.*

"Okay, what gives? I know something is different, but I don't know what. Tell me and put me out of my misery." Finley knew that wasn't completely true. Anything Whitt said couldn't ease the pain. But it served the purpose.

"We're officially engaged!" Whitt held up her left hand to show a sizeable, Asscher-cut diamond with baguettes. "We got the pictures and everything!"

"But I thought you were engaged before? I'm confused."

"We were, but because I took so long in deciding and laying out all the conditions, we never had a down-on-one-knee moment. So, he did it today. At the Taj Mahal!"

Finley jumped up and hugged her sister hard. *Whitt seemed blasé about this wedding. Until now.*

"Let me see the pictures!"

Whitt pulled out her phone and scrolled through the several pictures that they had taken in front of the Taj reflecting pool and on the plaza in front of the magnificent edifice. Some were taken by Darsh, some were selfies, but in all of them, Whitt's smile and David's look of adoration told the story. *Baby sis is getting hitched, for real.*

"Did you send Mama a picture yet?"

"Good gracious, in all the excitement, I forgot. I'd better send it now," Whitt said, taking back her phone. "There, it's done."

"And I'll give her ten seconds before she calls you to get the details!" Finley predicted.

Before she had finished the thought, Whitt's phone began to buzz. All she could hear after that was Mama's squeal and then a lot of chatter.

"Well, put us on speaker," Mama demanded when she realized Finley was in the room. "What exciting news. Now we have something to put in the paper to properly announce it. Until this, I was just focusing on the wedding, but now we can announce both the engagement and the wedding. And at the Taj Mahal, no less. How romantic!"

She went on, as Mama was wont to do. "You need to set a date. It is hard to do planning without a date. That will determine which venues are available as well as your colors and menu."

Mama began peppering Whitt with questions that Whitt had, until now, not thought about. The stricken look on Whitt's face suggested as much.

"Mama, let's just let her enjoy the moment. We can deal with that later, I promise," Finley said.

"Yes, of course, dear. And then we need to work on you and Max," Mama chuckled. "You need to get that boy down the aisle before both of you are wheelchair bound!"

Finley winced and forced a half smile. She needed to get off the phone before the conversation went too far, before she couldn't tread water anymore. "We'll see, Mama. For now, let's focus on Whitt. I need to get her some champagne to celebrate."

"Wait until I tell your father!" Mama said. "He will be so pleased. Let me let you go. I'm so happy for you, Whitt! My love to David."

When she had rung off, Whitt turned to Finley. "What was that about?"

"What?"

"That pained look when she mentioned Max. Don't think I didn't see. What happened?"

"Let's order some champagne and celebrate, kid. This about you, not me."

Finley fixed a smile and headed toward the phone to place the champagne order. As she recalled, they had the Billecart-Salmon that Whitt liked so much. They probably would need a couple of bottles once David came back.

"No, you're not getting out of this one. Something happened since we left, and you need to spill."

"Whitt, we can talk about it tomorrow. Nothing will have changed. Let's just be happy tonight."

"We can celebrate after you tell me what's going on." Whitt got to her feet and wrote David a quick note. She grabbed her key and phone and opened the door. "Come on. We're walking. You think better when you're moving."

Whitt pulled her sister outside, locked the door, and headed down the veranda to the green. The peacocks met them and escorted them to the gardens. Whitt kept a quick pace, partly to get away from places where other guests might be and partly to be sure that Finley followed her.

"You can slow down now. No one is chasing us," Finley joked.

She didn't really feel like laughing. She was hollowed out by the events of last night and today. The look on Max's face this afternoon haunted her. Her mind was a muddle of things she needed to do. She would have to postpone her flight. She couldn't leave now. She had to play along, to fake it until they got back to Delhi, so Whitt and David didn't know how serious the situation with Max was. She refused for this fiasco to be what Whitt and David remembered about their engagement.

"Okay, what gives? Talk to me." Whitt stopped and turned to face her sister.

"Only after you show me the ring. You hurried me out of there so fast, I didn't get a chance to see it in the light."

"Finley Walker Blake. You can see it later. Now you talk. What happened? Where is Max?"

"He's around. It's too complicated to try to explain. I don't even understand what's happening. All I know is I want out. I can't do this anymore. I don't want to do this anymore."

Finley was crying now. She sat down on a bench and watched the sun dipping behind the elaborate domes of the hotel. The peafowl, perhaps sensing her distress, crowded closer, brushing her legs with their plumes.

"Finley, start at the beginning."

"No, this is your day. I don't want to be the cause of it being less than truly memorable."

"It has been and will be a day I will never forget. But you are hurting. I can see it in your eyes, and I need to understand. So, tell me what's wrong."

Finley wiped her face on her shawl. "I don't even know where to start. I'm so confused. I can't figure out what started it. All I know is that Max walked out. He's sleeping on the couch. He's obsessed with there being something between me and Logan, but there isn't."

"David heard the same thing when he talked to Max. He tried to tell him that you guys are just friends."

"David talked to him?"

"Yeah, he found him in the bar last night. He was pretty soused. He still has it in his mind that there is something going on."

"He won't listen to reason. And if you had seen him today, you would have thought he was mad."

"What happened today?"

"I ran into Logan, Sandra, and Elise at the fort. The ladies went shopping, and Logan and I had lunch at the teahouse on the grounds. He wanted to talk about Hema. David was right. He likes her." Finley paused. "When we got back, Max must have seen us getting out of the car and jumped to all sorts of conclusions."

"What did he say?"

"'That didn't take you long' or something like that. But it was the look on his face. It was scary, and it just . . . it just cut me to the core."

"Finley, I am so sorry. I don't know what to say as I don't understand it any more than you do." Whitt hesitated before she continued, "I don't think he would hurt you, but I also don't think he is seeing things clearly right now. Why don't you sleep in our room tonight? Maybe in the morning, a way to sort this all out may be more apparent."

Finley stood to start walking again. The sun had dropped, and the lights had come on around the grounds. Spotlights shone on the trees and lit the walkways between the reflecting pools that centered the formal gardens. The peafowl were calling to each other, giving the gardens an eerie tranquility.

"I don't think it's going to get sorted out this time, Whitt. If you hadn't come back when you did, I would have been leaving in another hour for the airport. My bags are packed. I'm supposed to be on a 9:00 p.m. flight to Delhi."

"And then what? You just walk out and leave after everything you've invested in this relationship?"

"I don't know what else I can do. Talking to him about Logan is like talking to a brick wall. He sees what he sees and that is his 'fact.' What I say doesn't matter. He's obsessed with this. I can't deal with it."

"Maybe you could step away from your friendship with Logan. Give it some space."

"And let Max think he was right? That would give him carte blanche to dictate my friends, what I do with my time, my life. He would smother me. I'm too independent to live like that."

"So, you're just going to fold, huh? Aren't you the one always telling me you don't fold because you think you'll lose, you keep playing because you think you'll win?"

"Yep, I do. But I played my hand and I lost. I have to accept that. I keep going back to Max and hoping for a different outcome. Nothing changes. That's insanity, and I need to face it."

"Finley, what can I say or do to make it right?" Whitt wrapped her arms around her sister, holding her as if the struggle were hers.

"Logan asked the same thing," Finley laughed softly. "I have as well. I don't think there is much to be done. I need to mourn it and let it go." She started down the path again. "And I promise, for Mama's sake, I won't go crazy like I did last time."

Finley linked her arm through her sister's as they walked side by side between the reflecting pools. "What do you want as your colors? You need to decide quickly before Mama decides for you." Finley tried to lighten the mood.

They laughed at the possible color combinations that might most discombobulate their mother. Mauve and navy, too trite. Dusty rose and willow, too washed-out. Burgundy and peach, too garish. They had almost reached the end of the reflecting pools when Whitt saw something unusual.

"Finley, what is that?" Whitt pointed to something sticking out of the water.

Her sister moved closer to get a better look. Whitt grabbed her arm to pull her back, but curiosity got the better of her. Finley took a few steps forward and froze.

"Finley, what do you see? What is it? Finley!"

"It's Elise," Finley whispered. "I recognize the dress she had on. It's Elise."

Neither Whitt nor Finley could see a face. All that was visible was the lower portion of a torso and legs, which stuck out of the shallow water of the pool. Had it not been for the dress, it would have been impossible for the sisters to tell who it was.

"Do you have your phone on you?" Finley asked quietly. "I forgot mine in the room. We need to call the manager so he can call the police."

Whitt pulled out her phone and dialed the number for the hotel. The front desk answered and patched her to the resident manager.

"Mr. Patel, this is Whitt Blake in Room 5. I am with my sister, and we need you to come to the garden reflecting pool immediately."

The call continued. Finley could only hear snatches of the other side, but Whitt's responses made clear the flow of the conversation.

"No, this cannot wait, and no, this is not a matter for housekeeping, room service, or guest services. There is a body in the reflecting pool. That, I suggest, is a matter that only you, and the police, can attend to."

Patel and a security guard arrived at the reflecting pool in less than three minutes. The resident manager was trying to be inconspicuous, but his height and urgency of manner made stealth difficult. His saving grace was that most guests were in their rooms dressing for dinner, so few people were milling around.

"What has happened here?" Patel asked.

"We haven't a clue. We were walking in the gardens and came upon this. We don't know how long she has been here. I suggest you call the police. I don't think this is natural," Finley ventured.

Patel surveyed the area, making a point to stay as far away from the body as he could. He pulled his phone from his jacket pocket and dialed the number for Inspector Das. *Two murders on my watch. This is not going to be good for my career.*

"Until the police arrive, I suggest you ladies return to your rooms," the guard requested, while Patel explained the situation to Das on the phone. "I will escort you."

When they arrived at the rooms, David was already back. He looked confused by the presence of the security guard.

"What happened? Are you all right?"

"There has been an incident, sir. We are suggesting that the ladies stay in their rooms until the police arrive," the security guard said.

"Police? What's happened?" David's eyes grew wide.

"Let's get inside and we'll explain. And Finley, you are staying in here tonight!" Whitt declared.

Finley's protests fell on deaf ears. While Whitt explained to David what they had seen, Finley went to her room to collect her duffle and equipment. She took the time to cancel the car and her flight, knowing that the police were unlikely to let anyone leave the premises until this was solved.

She saw that the note she had put in the trash was now tucked back under the vase. "Gone for another run" was all it said. She knew what that meant. He was drunk, depressed, or both and hoped the run worked its magic and brought him back to normalcy. She knew too that he had seen her packed bags. She didn't care anymore. She was tempted to respond with a single word. "Gone." Instead, she crumpled the note and dropped in the trash.

WITHIN NO TIME, POLICE WERE everywhere. The inspector set up a command post in the office behind the reception desk and took over one of the hotel meeting rooms to conduct interviews. As soon as they'd arrived, a phalanx of officers had surveyed the area around the reflecting pools and found Elise's purse and "water" thermos. The contents of both the handbag and the thermos had been taken to the police station as evidence. From what the police could tell at first glance, there was no indication of foul play. Just Elise, with her head submerged in the reflecting pool and her feet pointing toward heaven.

Finley eventually made her way back to her sister's room, trying to delay making the move as long as she could but understanding her sister's motives. She had so wanted this day, and night, to be special for Whitt and David. That was hardly going to be possible with a guest on the couch.

Hoping to get her order in before the police shut down room service, Finley had requested that two bottles of Billecart be delivered immediately to her sister's room. *We're going to have an engagement celebration, murder or not. Mama would most definitely approve. You must soldier on in the face of adversity, she would say. Bolstered by a magnum, of course!*

The waiter had just left when she arrived. He had brought two buckets for icing. Either he had heard about the murder and was anticipating a shutdown or he was a man who thought ahead. She opened the leather folder that held the receipt, looking for the waiter's name. She would tip him appropriately later.

"What did you just do?" Whitt was grinning from ear to ear. "How did you arrange this with all that chaos outside? And so quickly!"

"Where there is a will, there is a way," Finley replied. She walked over to David and delivered a noisy kiss on his cheek. "Welcome to the clan, little brother!"

"Thanks. Not sure I want to be part of this tribe, though." David looked at Finley, eyebrow raised. "Every time you two are together, somebody dies!"

Finley and Whitt roared with laughter. "That is so true. Every time you have seen us together, there has been a body!" Whitt blurted between chuckles.

"Don't say that too loud or we'll be put under the Indian jailhouse, and that is one place I would like to avoid," her sister cautioned.

Finley opened the first bottle of champagne and passed the flutes around. She raised her glass to her sister and her future brother-in-law and wished them the best and happiest of marriages.

For a brief second, she dared to recognize that this was something she might never experience. Everyone else would find their someone and she would be left alone. If her history with Grant, her ex-husband, and Max was any indication, the thought held more than an element of truth. It saddened her, until she thought of all that she did have. Great family. Great friends. A great job. Great adventures. In all, a great life. It was too bad Max didn't want to be a part of it.

"So, now I am going to sound like Mama. Have you decided on a date yet?" Finley asked.

"We were talking about that in the car back. Between nodding off from exhaustion." Whitt couldn't stop smiling whenever she looked at David, and she was glancing at him often, as if to check that he wasn't a mirage.

"We know it'll be next year, simply because of schedules, but we were thinking early May. Your mother wants to have it in Charleston, and Whitt and I are okay with that."

"May will be a lot cooler. Good thinking." Finley nodded. "Better text that to Mama now or she will be on your hide, day and night, asking you to nail down a date."

"And I want celadon and peony pink for my colors!" Whitt was adamant. "With dove gray accents."

David laughed under his breath, and Finley let her mouth hang open as she fully grasped the decisions her sister had just made about something she'd had no interest in a mere twenty-four hours before.

"Stop gawping like that or you're going to catch flies!" Whitt snapped before quietly posing a question to the two. "Do you think Mama will allow me to have succulents in my bouquet?" Whitt looked like a child asking for seconds of ice cream.

"Whittaker, this is your wedding. Stop asking and just nicely tell Mama what you want." Finley got her sister's attention using her full name. Whitt have her a half laugh and nodded.

"You're right. I only plan to do this once, so I should have what I want." Whitt leaned over and kissed David. Their kiss was interrupted by urgent knocking on the door.

Finley and David both got up to answer it. Finley opened it, stepping behind to allow David to speak to whomever it was. She figured it was the police calling them for an interview. She was surprised when she heard Max's voice.

"Sorry to bother you, but have you seen Finley? I can't find her. And I saw all the police cars. Have you seen her?" He was breathless. His voice was frantic, almost pleading. She heard genuine concern. She wanted to reassure him with one hand and slap him with the other.

She stuck her head around the door as David stepped back to let Max in. "Come on in."

When Max was fully inside the room, Finley closed the door. He was still in his running clothes, the back of his T-shirt marked with sweat. Damp, dark curls drooped to almost cover one eye. He had been running, hard. She wondered how far he had gone. *And what the hell are you running from? You never seem to get away from whatever demon is chasing you. Maybe it's time to stand still and face it.*

David moved to stand beside Whitt's chair. He seemed to be giving Max space, but for what, Finley didn't know. Max looked from Finley's duffle, which had been dropped in the center of the room, to David and then to Finley. He said nothing. She stood watching him, saying nothing. David lowered himself onto the arm of Whitt's chair and observed the two. It was clear they were trying to figure out where to take this.

"Sorry, I didn't mean to interrupt," Max mumbled.

"You didn't," David said. "You want to join us for a drink?"

Max shook his head slightly. The sweat beads dropped from his hair. "I need to go take a shower. I ran."

The silence ate up the space between them. Finley hadn't said a word, but he could sense her presence, her eyes on the back of his head. He didn't dare turn around to face her just yet. David and Whitt were safer subjects of focus. Yet, he could feel her watching him. He wondered what she was seeing. Whether she could see what he felt right now. Scared, vulnerable, alone.

He turned around slowly. "I . . . I . . ."

His voice trailed off to silence. Words failed him. He was at a loss. He was lost. He swallowed hard. A deep sigh escaped his lips.

"Shall I get your bags for you?" was all he could think of. He prayed she wouldn't refuse.

Finley stared, searching his eyes, not sure what she would find. She drew a breath and then gave him a brief nod. Max walked to the center of the room and retrieved her duffle and equipment bag before turning for the door. He muttered a goodbye to Whitt and David and was gone.

"Are you going to be all right?" David asked. He was standing with his arm around Finley's shoulders. She nodded in response. She placed a kiss on his cheek and another on her finger, which she blew to her sister.

"Love you. Both," Finley said softly. "Thanks."

When Finley got to the room, Max was already in the shower. She could hear the water pulsing and imagined it beating onto his skin. Once, she had hopped in the shower after him and almost been knocked over by the force of the water. She wondered whether the hard-pulse nozzle that he always chose was a form of massage or self-flagellation. Now would not be the time to ask.

Max was towel-drying his hair when he walked back into the room. He had another towel wrapped around his waist. His chest was bare. Any other time, she would have smiled at the perfect symmetry of his body, the tautness of his stomach, shoulders, and back muscles, still, at almost forty. But today, the thought of him just made her sad.

He must have sensed her mood. "I better get dressed. The police will want to talk to each of us, I presume."

Finley simply nodded in reply. When he had dressed, he stood beside his side of the bed, looking at her as she read.

"Finley . . ."

"Not now, please. I don't want to talk tonight. I'm tired, and I still have to face the police," she whispered. "Please, not now."

He took his computer over to the sofa and sat down. He said no more.

Both were in their respective corners when the police knocked on the door. Max answered, but it was Finley they wanted. Both her and her sister.

"Why do you want to see them in particular?" Max asked. "Have you interviewed everyone else?"

"We are just beginning the interview process. We wanted to speak with the sisters first." The policeman signaled Finley to follow him. He knocked on Whitt's door and repeated the request.

Max was still puzzled. "Why do they want to talk to you two in particular?"

"Because we found the body," Finley announced, as she and her sister followed the officer down the corridor.

The meeting room that the police were using was one of the smaller meeting rooms in the hotel. It was well-appointed with a large mahogany table and cushioned armchairs, but the lighting was dim and cast shadows on the interrogating officer's narrow face. It was the same officer who had taken charge when the boy became ill. He had decided to interview the two sisters together. The two women sat across the table from the officer and another man, who sat obscured by the shadows.

"Good evening. My name is Inspector Dhruv Das. I hope we have not inconvenienced you too much. As you know, we have had another unfortunate incident here at the hotel, and we are trying to gather as much information as we can. I understand that you two found the woman who died."

"Yes, we did," Whitt answered.

"Why were you in the gardens?" the officer asked.

"We were taking a walk around the gardens and talking," Whitt responded.

"May I ask the subject of your conversation?"

"I fail to see how the subject of our conversation has any relevance," Whitt retorted.

The person in the shadows shifted his body slightly. Finley assumed it was a man because of his size. She recalled a similar interrogation in Morocco, in which the man in the shadows had turned about to be an Interpol inspector, who saved their lives. A tall man, he too had barely fit the chair.

"Whitt, I'm okay answering the question," Finley said. "I'd had a disagreement with my boyfriend, and I was talking through it with my sister."

"Ah. I apologize for the line of questioning, but I needed to determine its relevance and that could only come from knowing its nature." He inclined his head toward Whitt before continuing, "Then what did you do?"

"We were walking and talking as my sister said and then she noticed something unusual in the reflecting pool," Finley said. "We went to investigate and found Elise."

"And how did you know it was the woman who is called Elise?" the officer asked.

"From her dress. I had seen her earlier in the day, and she was wearing that dress."

"What was distinctive about the dress?"

Finley normally would have deferred to her sister on matters of fashion but given that Whitt had not seen Elise earlier in the day, her fashion sense was useless in this case. Finley tried to be as descriptive as possible, but all she could think about were the colors and the intricacy of the patterns in the fabric.

"It was an especially bright and expressive fabric. And the wrap across the bodice was well executed."

The officer smiled at the description. Finley didn't know if that was condescension or praise.

"Anything else distinctive?" the officer asked in a flat voice. He acted like he was bored with the conversation. *Well, it's your interrogation. If you're bored by it, it's because you aren't asking the right questions.*

"She always wore a lot of jewelry. I can't really remember what she had on today, but I think it was the large ruby that she generally wears with reds, and then a studded, cuff bracelet. I don't know which kind of stones. I wish my sister had been there. She knows stones." Finley cast a glance at Whitt with a smile.

"Did she always wear this particular piece, or did she make frequent changes in the pieces she wore?" a deep, resonant baritone asked from the shadows.

"Evans?" Finley and Whitt said at once, from voice recognition alone.

The officer turned in surprise and concern. He realized the man in the shadows' cover had been blown, and he wasn't sure what to do. The man in the shadows moved into the light and flashed a welcoming smile.

"If you promise not to say that name again until after this operation is over, I will acknowledge it. Here I am Darren Meadows, a millionaire with an eye for loose gems." Evans/Meadows rose and kissed both sisters.

"Das, I have had occasion to work with these two women before. They will help you immensely if we fill them in on what we're doing."

Das's brow furrowed. This was highly unusual, not at all the ways things were done here in India, which was by the book. But it was Evans's operation, so he deferred.

"The Jaipur police are working with Interpol on a series of jewel heists that may be part of a larger international operation. Someone is helping jewel brokers around the world gain access to stolen stones in fairly high volumes," the officer said.

"What we think is happening is that jewels are stolen and popped out of their settings and high-quality paste is substituted," Evans added. "Hotel guests at high-end establishments are especially vulnerable because they frequently wear a lot of jewelry and what they don't wear is in the safe in their room or in the security office, which is accessible to enterprising thieves."

"So, you think that someone was after Elise's jewels?" Finley asked.

"But why go after the ones she had on rather than raiding her room while she was out?" Whitt continued, "We were always out touring, so it would've been easier and safer."

"We don't know. That's why we're interviewing everyone," Evans said. "What do you know of the guests?"

Finley and Whitt went through each of the other guests they socialized with and what they knew about them, including what they had seen them do for the last three days. They described who had been on the tours with them and who had hung behind. Finley marveled at how much they had been able to pack into the three days since coming to Jaipur.

The inspector was scribbling furiously. He flipped back to pages periodically, apparently checking inconsistencies or gaps in the information, of which there were many.

"All we can say for sure is that both Elise and Sandra wore—and bought—a lot of jewelry. To be honest, if I wanted to make a killing—oops, sorry—if I wanted to hit the jackpot with jewels, I would have robbed Sandra, not Elise. Sandra had more and better jewels," Whitt said.

"Maybe she's next," Finley posited. "You may want to keep an eye on Sandra to be sure she's safe. The real question is whether the killer is someone who came into the hotel from the outside or someone who was already among us inside."

DAS, WITH EVANS NOW RETURNED to the shadows, interviewed the remaining guests, including Max and David. Having just begun their investigation, they asked that all guests stay on the hotel grounds until further notice. While Ravi and Devya protested what Devya called "house arrest," the other guests understood the need for the restrictions. That the police would allow the polo matches to take place eventually mollified Ravi.

By the time the last interview had concluded, Evans was exhausted, more mentally than physically. He had been working with senior officers of the Jaipur police for almost three months, since he was released from convalescence. It had taken over a month for his ribs to heal after the incident in Sri Lanka. He was slow getting back into action. This assignment had seemed an easy way to ease back into work—until someone started killing off people. He wondered whether there had been one victim, Elise, or two. He was still searching for the connection between this murder and the death of the houseboy.

From what he could tell, the boy's death was truly an accident. While the police had not been able to find any evidence of the sedative that he had ingested among the hotel guests' belongings, it seemed too far a stretch to believe that an outside agent had come into the hotel for the sole purpose of hurting the boy. Unless the purpose was to hurt someone else and the boy was just collateral damage. He would let that idea rest in his mind for a while and see what developed. Right now, he needed a drink.

After helping Das with his notes, Evans headed toward the bar. He had booked himself into the hotel under the name of Meadows in order to get closer to the guests. He wasn't convinced that one of them had committed the murder, but the only way to find out was to mingle with them and see whether anything new came to light.

Walking toward the Polo Club, he spotted Finley. She was at one of the tables on the far side of the open-air terrace. It was late, and the rest of the tables were empty. He watched her as she leaned her head on the back of her chair and surveyed the canopy of bright stars above her. She remained in that position for a while, moving only slightly to zero in on another constellation. He smiled at both the simplicity of her gesture and the beauty of the woman making it. He sighed deeply. As he approached, she looked up and smiled.

"Come and keep me company," she called. "I realized when I left you that I hadn't eaten since lunch. Please join me. I'll never be able to finish all this."

"Thanks. I'll take you up on that." Evans signaled the waiter for another place setting and ordered a beer when he came with the plate and silverware. "Where's your sister?"

"She went back to her room. She got engaged today! So, she went to be with David."

"Was that what your tiff with Max was about? 'Where's *my* ring?'" Evans smiled. "You can tell me I am prying, if you want."

"No. I would never confront Max like that! Whiny women are tiring. Truth is that we argued before they left for Agra." Finley sipped her wine and pulled at the piece of roti on her plate.

"Do you want to talk about it?"

"Not really. At least not yet." Finley redirected the conversation, "So, do you have any suspects for Elise's murder? And you can tell me if I'm prying."

Evans laughed. "That's fair. We don't have any suspects. We're still trying to piece together what happened."

"To tell you the truth, when I first saw her, I thought she had gotten drunk, fallen in the pool, and drowned!

"Why would you think that?" Evans was puzzled. "Was she frequently drunk?"

"She was sozzled all the time." Finley laughed wryly. "She always had her 'water' thermos with her, but water was the least thing in it."

"What did she normally drink?"

"Gin and tonics. With a twist. She was very particular about how she wanted her drink made. She made that clear the first day she got here."

"And did she have any problem getting the staff to adhere to her request?"

"No. From the first day, they seemed to know what she liked and kept her well supplied."

"What do you mean?"

"Her thermos was always filled. They would bring her one at breakfast and she would pour it into the thermos and then refill it if she came to the restaurant for lunch or tea."

"Was it the same waiter that always brought it?"

"That I can't say."

"You said she and another woman always wore a lot of jewelry. Could you tell if it was real?"

"I couldn't, but I'm sure Whitt could. If it was paste, it was a good copy. The stones caught the light well from what I could see."

"Humph!" Evans said. His eyes narrowed. He was thinking, probably pulling puzzle pieces from his mental drawers and trying to arrange them into a plausible pattern.

"What?" Finley was watching him closely now. Observing the concentration that caused the brief separation between his hooded eyes to narrow, like a hawk just before it strikes. The pursing of his mouth that ended with a half curl of his lip. The movement of his long, tapered fingers around the base of his beer as he absent-mindedly wiped away the condensation, leaving beaded stripes on the glass.

"I'm just trying to figure out what parts of our theory have validity. And how, or whether, the boy's death plays into this."

"You'll figure it out. You always do," Finley observed. She wanted to change the conversation. The talk of death was depressing her. "So, you decided to come to Delhi to recover?"

She was talking about the last time she and Whitt had seen Evans. They had been in Sri Lanka on holiday and had found Evans near death in a cupboard in the hotel in which they were staying. They had tended his injuries with the help of some friends on the island, enough that his team could transport him to safety. In the process, they solved the murders of three of Evans's agents. At that time, he had said he would try to make it back to Lyon to recover, unless it became impossible to make the trip. Then Delhi would have to do.

"They needed me to 'stay dead' for a while longer and figured India was a rather good place to get lost. So, I hung out in Goa for a month or so."

"You were pretty bad off when they picked you up. We weren't sure you were going to make it."

Evans reached across and tapped Finley's arm. "Oh, ye of little faith. Surely, I am made of sturdier stuff than that."

"You didn't see what you looked like when we found you!"

"True. Honestly, I don't know that I would have made it through another night without medical attention. I have you and Whitt to thank for finding me and patching me back together."

"That was Lita and Anu, not us." Finley grew serious, remembering how badly injured Evans had been. "In any case, you survived."

"And you? How are you surviving?" Evans again touched her arm, but this time, he left his hand in place. It was only the bellman calling his name that prompted him to remove it.

"Mr. Meadows. Sir, there is a message for you." Evans tipped the man and opened the envelope. He read in silence, drawing in a breath and sighing when he had finished reading. He stared at some random object on the table, his brow furrowing again.

"It appears that your friend, Elise, was poisoned. Viper venom was found mixed with the content of the thermos. And yes, it was gin and tonic with a twist. The lime must have masked the taste of the venom. It is unlikely that she put it there or that it got there accidentally, confirming our suspicion of murder."

Finley recoiled at Evans's pronouncement. "Who would want to do such a thing? That is such a horrible way to die! And why?"

"That I don't know, but I intend to find out," Evans said. He paused and caught her eye. "But that doesn't mean you are off the hook telling me how you are."

"I'm okay. Just going through a few changes." Finley grew quiet. "Max and I going through a rough spot."

"I'm sorry. I'm sure it will work out."

"I'm not so sure this time," Finley muttered.

"Surely, he isn't cheating on you!"

Finley gave a half laugh. "No, he thinks I'm cheating on him."

"Where did he get that from? I can understand him knowing that you could have a line out the door of men interested in you. But what made him think that you would take any of them up on it?"

Finley explained Logan and his role in the misunderstanding. "He helped me keep it together when Max and I broke up the first time. Logan and I tried it for a while, but we both decided we were better as friends. And he has been a dear friend ever since."

"And Max thinks that something is going on now?"

"Yeah, he basically accused me of betraying him." Finley gulped to swallow the tears that threatened to well up.

"You have got to be kidding me!" The tears creeping down Finley's cheek told Evans otherwise.

"Nope. He has it in his head that I'm lying to him," Finley said. "He's obsessed with the idea."

Evans sat straighter in his chair and directed his hawklike gaze at Finley. "He hasn't hurt you, has he?"

"No, he would never do that. But he isn't himself. He can't let it go, regardless of what I or anyone else tells him."

"I am not one qualified to give advice in this area, but Max is a fool," Evans started. "And so are you."

"I can't disagree. I keep walking away and then going back and submitting myself to the same thing again and again. Not too rational."

Evans paused, his fingers steepled. He waited until she had looked up and engaged him. "Do you love him?"

Finley drew a deep breath. She couldn't deny that after everything that had happened, at the end of all the anger and frustration and confusion and hurt was a profoundly deep and unshakable love for the man. She really must be crazy. No rational person would do what she had done, yet again, just this evening. *I'm not crazy, just stupid in love. I've got to admit it.* She returned Evans's gaze and nodded with a shy smile.

"Then fight for him. We've established that he's not too smart or he would have taken you off the market long ago. That and the fact that he's angry with other men for noticing what he has failed to claim should be sufficient proof." She and Evans shared a laugh.

He continued, "That said, it is clear to me that he loves you. So, he can't be so dumb."

Finley gave Evans a sad smile as she acknowledged the truth in what he had said. She checked her watch. "Goodness, it's late and you must be exhausted. I'll get the check."

"No, this is on me," Evans said. "I think I'll have a nightcap before I turn in. Sleep tight."

Finley got to her feet and walked over to Evans's chair. She took his face in her hands and kissed him gently on the forehead. "Thank you."

When she raised her head, her eyes met Max's glare. He paused for a moment before stalking off toward their room.

In the morning, Max acted as if nothing had happened the night before. He waited until she got dressed and escorted her to breakfast. From all appearances, things were back to normal. Finley was confused. She had no idea what had changed, if anything, but she played along. Whitt raised an eyebrow, questioning the situation, to which Finley gave a noncommittal shrug.

Whitt and David had claimed a small, round table away from the main dining area. It was just as well, in Finley's opinion. She didn't want to have to answer questions about Elise and the circumstances of her death. She also didn't want to hear further speculation about what had happened. The police would deal with it. She had enough problems of her own.

"The guy with Logan looks an awful like Evans. Is it?" David asked with a slight jerk of his head in Evans's direction.

Evans had joined Logan at his table, which also included Ravi, Devya, and Sandra. Finley suspected that he was playing the gregarious millionaire to get a better read on the guests at the hotel. Having heard their interviews, he had a head start in probing what they knew and more importantly, she thought, how they came to know it.

Whitt responded in a neutral whisper. "Yes, but he's called Darren Meadows and is a rich guy who likes shiny baubles."

"You knew he was here?" David's voice pitched at the revelation. "When were you going to fill me in?"

"When Evans gave us the okay," Whitt shot back. Finley could see where this conversation was going. From David's view, Whitt's loyalty to divulge everything should rest with him. Whitt clearly saw it differently.

"Oh, I see." David tried to modulate his voice to mask his hurt, but hurt he was.

Whitt turned to face David before saying, "Look, sweetheart, I don't know what this thing is that Evans is working on, but when he asks me to play along, I do. When he asks me to stay mum, I do. He has saved our tushes too many times for me not to."

She paused and put her hand on David's. "On everything else, I am an open book. I swear."

David ended the conversation with a kiss. He turned his attention to the others. "What's on the agenda today, besides polo? You guys are going, aren't you?"

"It depends on Finley," Max said, looking over at her as he spoke.

Finley had noticed that for the last few days, almost since the tension with Logan began, he had stopped calling her Fin, as he normally did, and had reverted to a more formal form of her given name. It felt like a stab every time she heard it. Like a little prod that was pushing them further and further apart.

"I figured I would make an appearance. Not too sure I want to stand in the hot sun and watch the matches, but I'm sure we can find shade somewhere on the grounds."

"Of course you're going, you silly goose," Whitt said. "When have we ever passed up and opportunity to wear frilly dresses, sport large picture hats, and drink champagne all afternoon?"

"When you put it that way, who would ever pass up the chance?" Finley expressed mock indignation and smiled at her sister. "Which means another shopping expedition, doesn't it?"

"Bien sûr, my dear," Whitt said. "We'll send the boys off somewhere to work or watch football while we see what we have in the shops. The shops here at the hotel will only be open until noon, so we have to be quick."

"What time does this thing start?" Max asked with little enthusiasm.

"The first match is at two. On the green at the far end of the property," David replied.

"Far away from the reflecting pools, let's hope," Whitt added.

"Yeah, they have that area cordoned off," Max reported. "When I went for my run this morning, the staff was directing people to the other side of the building."

Whitt took a quick glance at her watch and pulled her sister to her feet. "It's getting late. Grab your bag. We need to be off."

She leaned in to kiss David goodbye. Finley simply raised her hand in farewell and started off. Max clenched his jaw but nodded in reply.

"Still no better?" Whitt asked, as they headed toward one of the dress shops.

"I don't know. At least he can be in my presence without snarling at me."

"He'll come to his senses soon enough. Just give him some space."

He will have all the space he needs when I'm gone.

DESPITE THEIR FEAR THAT THE hotel dress shop would have a limited selection, both Finley and Whitt were able to find dresses that they liked for the polo matches later that afternoon. Whitt had settled on a grass linen sheath in a celery-green-on-cream abstract print. Finley had surprised herself and opted for a silk chiffon, high-necked, floral halter dress with tiny ruffles at the hem that flounced when she walked. She had decided a new dress was in order to counter her sour mood. When she put this one on, she had found herself smiling.

The hats were more of a trial, however. The sisters spent a good hour trying and retrying a selection of outrageous picture hats before settling on a couple of floppy, straw hats. While the shop assistant worked on finding and attaching the right hat ribbons to match their dresses, Finley and Whitt went around to the jewelry store next door.

"Don't you even think of buying anything here," Finley whispered under her breath. "You have enough jewelry in your room to adorn a maharani!"

"I was just looking," Whitt pouted.

"I know you. You never just look."

Whitt peered into the case, looking up to engage the attendant behind the counter. "Where do most of the stones that you carry come from?"

"From India, Sri Lanka, Burma, all over the world," the young man attending them said. "We sell only the finest gems here."

Whitt went on, "Do you provide a certificate of authenticity for the stones? One can never be too sure about getting the real thing."

"But of course, madame," the assistant said indignantly. "We stand behind our stones."

"I'm sure you do," Finley tried to assure him. "My sister was just concerned about buying jewelry overseas. We've heard of cases where fakes were passed off as real." She continued, "Do many visitors buy jewelry to take home with them?"

"Oh, yes, ma'am. Many of our guests buy jewelry or unset stones from us to take home to the US and Europe. Many Asians also buy from us. Indian stones are first-class."

"Do you ship stones as well?"

"If you wish, madame, we can ship them. We have shipping companies that we regularly use."

"Well, I will talk to my husband and see what he says. Thank you so much." Finley flashed a big smile and pulled her sister out of the store.

"What was that about? *Your husband!* I go in and you start asking questions." Whitt was looking at her sister like she had horns.

"I will tell you later. Just take a look—slowly, use the mirror—at the guy behind the curtain in the back." Finley positioned her sister so that she could pretend to look in an adjacent shop window and use the mirror there to look back into the jewelry store.

Whitt saw a large, bearded man, but his position behind the curtain obstructed her view of his features.

"Let's go get our purchases and head to the room." Finley led the way back into the dress shop.

When they got back to Whitt's room, Whitt closed the door and confronted her sister.

"Are you going to tell me what that was about? It was like Jekyll and Hyde back there, with you playing both parts!"

"The man you saw back there was the same guy who was talking to Ravi at the boat dock a few days ago," Finley said. "When you started talking about certificates of authenticity, I got the idea that the guys Evans was talking about might use legitimate jewelry stores somehow to ship the stones out."

She dropped down into her favorite easy chair and kicked off her shoes. "Admittedly, it was a crazy idea. And the pieces still don't fit. I need to just leave it. It's not as if I don't already have enough on my mind."

"You can tell Evans later. But now you need to bring your stuff over here and let's get dressed together. David can get dressed with Max."

David was none too pleased at having to grab his clothes and Dopp kit and cart it over to Max's room, but he wasn't in the mood for an argument, so he complied. And when, sometime later, he and Max knocked on the door, he had even less to complain about.

"My, my, my! Don't you ladies look lovely." David stood back to allow Whitt and Finley to step out onto the veranda. Whitt had paired her dress with nude, stack-heeled sandals, while Finley had gone with low-heeled, beige, ribbon-wrapped wedges. Whitt must have coordinated her outfit with David since he was sporting cream-colored linen pants with a stonewashed, olive, linen jacket. They were a matched pair.

Finley smiled approvingly at Max in spite of herself. *Damn, why does he have to be so easy on the eyes?* He wore his signature marine blue linen blazer with white linen pants and shirt. In his breast pocket, he had stuck a pale-blue pocket square. He offered her his arm, and she caught the teal of his eyes on her when she reached to take it.

"You look beautiful," he whispered wistfully. "As always."

Finley and Max let Whitt and David carry the conversation. They followed along in silence across the acres of carefully manicured parade field. Finley had seen turbaned men on horseback execute intricate maneuvers on the field during the evening "changing of the guards." Now they stood watch as guests from outside the hotel surged onto the field for the matches.

Logan and Sandra stood with Ravi and his wife under a sun canopy, champagne in hand. They appeared to be making the best of the situation, considering Elise's recent death. Under different circumstances, Finley would have gone to greet them with kisses and hugs. Today she hung back, waiting for Whitt to determine the direction. Whitt, sensing the tension, headed straight for the champagne tent. *If I must play mediator all afternoon, at least let me do it well-fortified,* Whitt thought.

Finley scanned the crowd as she sipped her champagne. All the glitterati of Jaipur had turned out. Every cricket star, Bollywood starlet, or business tycoon within a hundred-mile radius was there. She was surprised how many foreigners there were in the city. But given Jaipur's population, there were bound to be a few, and events like this seemed to attract expats.

Finley stood, surveying the grounds halfheartedly. Whitt and David were chuckling about something—or someone—but she and Max didn't even try to initiate conversation. Just being was hard enough. She put down her empty flute and pulled out her camera.

"I'm going to go see if I can get some shots of the players and their ponies before they start."

"I'll go with you," Whitt said. David and Max declined the invitation to join, so the two sisters struck off for the stables.

Some minutes later, his champagne finished, Max was feeling restless. "If you don't mind, David, I think I'll roam around a bit. I'll meet you back here before the first match. I know the girls will want more champagne after their trip to the stables."

David laughed and nodded. "See you in a while."

Max wandered among the crowd. He wanted to be by himself, but not alone. He was unsettled by the events of the past few days. His disagreement with Finley, his anger at her failure to see his point of view, his sense of isolation, the murders, Logan, Evans. He wished things could be like they were before. Normal.

He had just reached the far end of the field when he heard his name. He turned to see Logan walking slowly toward him. He stopped.

"Max . . ."

"Logan, stay out of it." Max wasn't in the mood for having a conversation with anyone, let alone Logan, especially when he knew what the subject would be.

Logan faced him, one hand casually in his pocket. He was trying hard to keep the anger out of his voice. He didn't want this to escalate, for Finley's sake.

"I can't. Look, I don't know what's going on, but something is, and she's hurt by it."

Max curled and unfurled his fist several times before he spoke. "Don't act the innocent. You two say you're just friends, but I know there's more."

"Is that what this is all about? Still?" Logan shook his head in disbelief. "The notion that there is something between us, besides friendship, is absurd." He stepped forward. "Man, if there was *any* chance, I would be all over it. But she made it clear that we're only friends, and I respect that because I care about her. I want her to be happy."

Max started to respond, but Logan stopped him. He took another step forward so that he and Max were eye to eye.

"You're a damn fool if you can't see how much she loves you. There's nothing more to be said. Just a damn fool." He turned and walked back through the growing mass of people, toward the grandstand. Max watched him until he was lost in the crowd.

Max found the rest of the Four Musketeers in front of the champagne station. Whitt and David had another glass in hand.

Finley was taking pictures of random people while they talked. She didn't look as if she was paying much attention to her work. Her usual focus wasn't there. No turning of the head or narrowing of her eyes. No checking of the light or the angle. She was just aiming and clicking.

"Did you get some good shots of the riders?" he asked.

"Yes, the players and trainers were quite accommodating." The response sounded as stilted as it felt to say. Finley returned the camera to her eye. *After all these years and I feel awkward around him. That can't be good. I just want to go home.*

"She has some funny ones of a dog drinking from one of the horse's champagne buckets," Whitt recounted in an attempt to shift the rhythm, lift the mood. "I hope they mixed it with a lot of water, or those poor animals are going to be looped."

Max smiled stiffly. "You'll have to show them to me when we get back to the room. Look, there are some seats in the grandstand farther down, if you want to sit." David nodded and led the way.

The view from the grandstand was a good one. The foursome could see all the action. Finley could see why the transition from this to elephant polo had been so easy for the Sri Lankans. The rules and the chukka structure were mirror images.

"So, who do you think did it this time?" Whitt leaned over and whispered to her sister.

"Did what?" Finley's attention was riveted on the play taking place on the field. During a break in the play, she diverted her eyes for a second to Whitt.

"The murder!" she mouthed.

"Whitt, it's a little inappropriate to be playing murder when we have real ones on our doorstep, unsolved."

"I know, but the setting and all these people are just too good to pass up."

Finley cast an eye at Max beside her, who was engrossed in the match. David was as well. She relented.

"Who and how?" she whispered, her eyes forward.

"The man on the sidelines in the fedora with the plaid band. Over the side at the Amber Fort."

"Goodness! You could fall there, and if someone wasn't looking for you, you could rot for days."

Max touched her arm and then, realizing what he had done, quickly withdrew it. "I thought you called me. Sorry."

Finley looked up and shook her head. "I was talking to Whitt."

Whitt hadn't seen the exchange and continued with clues. But Finley could still feel the warmth of his hand on her bare skin. That one touch had ignited a barrage of emotions. Connection, confusion, comfort, and sadness. Most of all, sadness.

She turned her attention back to her sister. *I can't keep playing like everything is all right. It's exhausting me and isn't making it hurt any less. He's still angry. I'm still hurt. I just want to go home.*

Finley gave her sister a plausible killer for this round of the Murder Game and returned her attention to the field. On the far side of the field, Devya was maintaining her posture of ennui, leaning against the barrier and appearing more interested in the condition of her nail polish than what was happening on the field. Every time she flipped her hair back, the man with whom her husband was talking looked over and smiled slyly.

Ravi did not appear to be pleased with the way the conversation was going. His hand jerked back and forth as he seemingly tried to explain something to the man, but it was clearly not being understood or accepted. This man was tall, like the man at the dock had been, but clean-shaven. He was well-dressed in a taupe linen suit and French blue shirt. *Perhaps another of the Chosen Ones from the first families. Maybe this is just a family squabble. But this guy looks as if he would settle the score like the Corleones.*

Finley reached into her bag and pulled out her camera. She took a few shots of the horses, which thundered past her toward the goal, before shifting her focus to the opposite side of the field. The man was still there, and he and Ravi were still discussing.

At one point, when Ravi shrugged in response to something the man had said, the man firmly took Ravi by the shoulder and shook his head slowly. *Clearly, ignorance is not an excuse in this man's mind. Whatever is being negotiated, Ravi is at a disadvantage.* When, minutes later, Logan entered the frame and began to talk to Devya, the man whispered something in Ravi's ear and walked away.

Finley mentally made a note to ask Logan what he saw and heard of the conversation but then thought better of it. The last thing she needed was a full-on blowout between Max and Logan because of a casual question. Max was seething beneath the surface. She didn't want to be the one that took him to the breaking point.

With a look, Max made it known that it already may have been too late for that. Max had followed her lens across the field and set his eye on Logan and Ravi in conversation. He looked at Logan and then turned slowly to give Finley a knowing side-glance before bringing his attention back to the match.

At the interval, Finley followed Max over to the refreshment tent. Whitt and David had managed to slip away as the group negotiated the crowds. Finley was tired and heartsick. She needed to get away. She didn't want to playact anymore.

"Look, this sun has really taken it out of me. If you don't mind, I think I'll walk back to the room," she said.

Max glanced at her with concern. "Do you want me to walk you back?"

Finley gently shook her head and instinctively kissed him on the cheek. He stood, following her with his eyes as she walked across the green, hat in hand. He was so absorbed by her that he neither saw nor heard Evans when he came up.

"Don't blow my cover. In case they didn't tell you, I'm Darren Meadows. Remember we met over breakfast? Take the champagne and thank me for it," Evans muttered in a low voice.

Max did as he was told, his eyes still on Finley as he sipped. Evans joined him in his surveillance of her until she disappeared around the building.

"You're a fool." Evans finally broke the silence.

"Well, hello to you, too! That's the second time today someone has called me that. At least there's consistency," Max said sardonically.

"Seems to me if you have two independent sources confirming the same truth, there is a high probability that there is veracity." Evans had turned to face him now.

His voice softened. "For heaven's sake, man, don't hurt her again. She has been through enough. If you can't commit to her, then leave her for someone who can."

"Who, you?" Max snapped.

"No. I was man enough to bow out long ago. A decision I will perpetually regret."

Both men returned to taking in the crowd. Finding little there to talk about and nothing more to say, they remained silent. It was Evans who interrupted the quiet again.

"Max, I know we aren't friends, and probably never will be, so if I'm out of line, so be it. But Finley is a very special woman. Who happens to love you. Very much. You've got to stop dancing with ghosts, or you are going to lose her. I don't know who betrayed you before, but it wasn't Finley. Stop punishing her for something she didn't do."

Evans set his glass on the tray of a passing waiter, turned, and left.

12

FINLEY WALKED BACK ACROSS THE green, enjoying the solitude and the warm afternoon sun on her skin. She knew Whitt would be disappointed that she had left. Whitt had been in a strange humor since her engagement. She was almost giddy at times, unlike her normal disposition, which was reserved and wary. Finley knew that, had she been there, Whitt would have enjoyed another round of the Murder Game, however inappropriate, as well as a verbal joust with mercurial Devya, just for the hell of it. *You're on your own, baby sis.*

For her part, Finley was conflicted. She was indeed Dr. Jekyll and Mr. Hyde. On the one hand, she was running through the things she needed to remember to take to her new place, wherever that was, when she moved out of Max's apartment. And yet, on the other, she was plumbing the depths of the loss she would feel without him in her life. She had experienced that before and it had almost sent her mad. *Lord, what are you trying to teach me with this pain? Whatever it is, I am not getting it.*

She stopped on her trek back to the room and leaned on the column of one of the buildings. She had never felt so adrift, so unmoored. She had neither a steady job nor a permanent home because her anchor had been Max. And now that was gone. *Finley, you have got to stop wallowing. It is what it is. Put on your big-girl pants and get on with it.*

She was almost at the portal that led to her corridor. At first, she thought it was the television in one of the rooms. It sounded like the fight scene from an action movie. Furniture was moving about a room. Dishes were breaking. There was scuffling and the sounds of people in combat. The grunts and cries and cursing. But it took her only a second to realize that the scream she heard was real, not staged.

She ran up the stairs and listened again. The ruckus was coming from Sandra's room.

"Sandra! Sandra! Are you all right?" Finley called out loudly as she banged on the door. Realizing that it was open, she barged in. "Sandra!"

The room had been tossed, as if by a hurricane. Sandra lay on the floor, buried by clothes and bedding and bric-a-brac from the sitting room. From the corner of her eye, Finley could see movement as whoever it was that had broken in made a hasty retreat onto the terrace and over the railing.

"Sandra. Are you okay? What happened?" Finley was on her knees, trying to assess the extent of Sandra's injuries. "Let me get someone to help you."

She quick dialed the front desk. "I need security and a doctor to Mrs. Sandra Ruiter's room. No, I don't know the room number. This is an emergency. Look it up. She has been attacked. Send security!"

Finley realized she was spitting out directives without any punctuating pleasantries. She would apologize for her abruptness later. She ran to the bathroom and wet a towel to stem the blood flowing down Sandra's face.

When she got back, Sandra had thrown off the things that had buried her and pulled herself into an upright position. She took the towel Finley offered with a sad smile and applied it to her head.

"Thank you. I think you just saved me. From what, I don't know. But I think it was going to get bad." Tears diluted the blood that ran down her cheek.

"Don't try to talk," Finley said. "I called for a doctor. They should be here shortly. Just rest."

"Did they take everything?" Sandra winced as she turned her head to survey the room. "They were looking to rob me, I think."

"From what I could see, they left empty-handed. Unless they had a bag—"

Her last thought was interrupted by a barrage of security and policemen storming the suite.

"Which way did they go?" someone shouted.

Finley pointed to the terrace as the means of escape in hopes that they might be caught quickly and the matter resolved. She knew that was unlikely, but she wanted closure on something, and this incident seemed easiest.

"Are you ladies hurt? What happened?" The security guard lobbed questions at the two women. Sandra, still in shock, looked at him blankly.

"Mrs. Ruiter was attacked. She can give you more details after she is seen by a doctor. Is one coming? I asked for one when I put in the call to the desk," Finley said.

"Yes, ma'am. The doctor is coming."

Almost on cue, the doctor, a man in his late fifties with kind eyes and a comforting manner, entered and began ministering to Sandra. He asked her questions in a low, quiet voice that protected her privacy even as he elicited the information that he needed to treat her. She was still in shock, answering the doctor's questions in a monotone voice, her eyes staring off into space.

"How did you come to be here?" one of the policemen asked Finley, who had moved into the sitting room to give the doctor more space.

"I was passing and heard Mrs. Ruiter scream. I called out to her and that must have scared the robbers off," Finley replied. "I don't know any more than that."

"Please wait here until we secure the area and the inspector comes," the policeman directed.

Finley complied. While she waited, she decided to contact Evans. This wasn't a random robbery. That much she knew. She hoped Evans would agree. She dialed the WhatsApp number she had been given over a year ago in Tangier, when she and her sister had been kidnapped.

"Mr. Meadows, this is Finley Blake. We met yesterday." Finley tried to keep her voice low in case any of the security or police were listening.

She stuck her head out the door to grab the room number. "Look, I'm in Sandra's room, Room 28, on the back side of the building looking onto the gardens. I want to show you something. I think you might find it interesting. If you are available immediately. Great."

When Evans arrived at the door, Finley wondered what story he would give in order to gain entrance. He couldn't use his Interpol credentials, and there would be little reason for him to be there, in Sandra's room, but for his work.

"Darling, are you hurt badly?" Evans swept into the room and headed directly to Sandra. He dropped to one knee, taking her hand in his and kissing it gently. "Did they hurt you, sweetheart? I should have been here to protect you."

Sandra stared at him, bewildered.

"You mustn't talk until the doctor has completely checked you over." Evans stood and looked endearingly at Sandra. "Does she have a concussion or any serious injury?"

The doctor, assuming some relationship between the two, began explaining the nature of Sandra's injuries to Evans.

"She is just shaken up. The blood came from a small head wound that must have occurred when she was pushed. Head wounds always look worse than they are. Nothing serious. I gave her a mild sedative to help her sleep," the doctor said.

The resident manager had entered shortly after Evans arrived. Seeing the condition of the room, he had arranged to move her to an identical suite next door.

"The room has been prepared. She can be moved now so she can rest," he said solicitously. "Once the police have finished in here, we will send an attendant to help her sort through her things and we will have them moved at that time."

He gave a small bow and proceeded to give instructions to the staff that stood attentively at the door. As Sandra was escorted over, Patel returned to Finley and Evans.

"Lest you think that this sort of thing happens frequently at the Rambaugh, please let me assure you that, in my ten years here, we have never had such an incident. I am so sorry that your stay has been marred by these unfortunate circumstances. We will make it up to you. I promise."

He again gave a small bow and backed out of the door.

"Let's step outside," Evans said to Finley, as he steered her to the portico.

"What happened?" he asked, when they were away from the police and security still milling around the room.

"You aren't going to tell them to stop trampling on evidence?" Finley looked over his shoulder at the swarm of people in the room, wandering about.

"I don't have any authority. I put an emergency call into Das, but it will take him a while to get here from across town. Not much I can do."

"I can take pictures at least." Finley grabbed her camera from her bag and headed back into the room.

She first took a panoramic shot of the whole room and then started taking photos section by section of the room. Evans directed her at times to specific areas or pieces of clothing. The place had been pretty much tossed. Drawers were opened. The contents of bags and purses were dumped on the sofa and floor. Even the lining of one of Sandra's suitcases had been slashed. When she finished in the bedroom, she moved to the sitting room and, finally, to the terrace.

She remembered the path the robbers had taken and took detailed pictures of those areas. There were no visible footprints or nicks on the railing to suggest the exact route they had used. She was glad she had caught a glimpse of them, or she would have had no idea of how they exited. As she leaned over to track their activity out the terrace and over the railing, she spied something shiny in the underbrush below Sandra's terrace.

"Come with me," Finley said. No one was paying attention to their actions. Security had left, and the remaining police appeared to be waiting for instructions.

At the bottom of the stairs, she turned toward the back of the building, which opened onto an inner courtyard. She pointed to the lush landscaping that trimmed the area. Evans leaned over and stuck his hand into the bush that Finley pointed out. It had been hard to see it from the ground, but there in the underbrush was a large, black messenger bag.

"Grab a shot of it before I pick it up," Evans requested.

Finley took several pictures from a few different angles. When she had finished, Evans pulled the bag from its hiding spot and looked inside. The bag was filled almost to the bursting point with necklaces, bracelets, and small sacks of raw stones. Finley wondered whether this was all Sandra's or whether the burglars had hit other guests during their spree.

"I don't know whether they hid it or dropped it, but I think there is a pretty big stash here of stolen items. Are these all Sandra's?" Evans clearly had the same questions.

"I don't know. I do know that she has been buying jewelry like there's no tomorrow since we got here. But I don't recall that she bought that many raw stones. That said, we weren't always together."

"I'll turn this over to Das and he can go through it with her once she wakes up." Evans zipped up the bag and threw it over his shoulder.

Finley gently tapped his arm as he passed on his way back upstairs. He turned and looked at her quizzically.

"What was with the scene up there?" Finley asked, her lip creeping into a smile. "Were you playacting or do Darren Meadows and Sandra have something going on?"

Evans laughed. "Was I that convincing? I couldn't think of any other way to get in." He paused and gave her a wink. "Rest assured, my dear. My heart belongs to you."

By the time they got back to the room, Das had arrived. He was trying to organize his squad and get evidence gathered even as he assessed the scene. The room was as they had left it. Policemen still milled around as if unsure what to do next, even after receiving instruction from their superior officer.

"This is a disaster!" Das was shaking his head. He kept raking his fingers through his hair as he walked through the mess of dishes, clothes, and bedding that was strewn on the floor. "They preserved nothing! Nothing!"

Evans scanned the room again and shook his head. He had to agree. They were unlikely to find any viable evidence in what was lying around. He probably held the best evidence in his hand. He held out the bag. "Not everything is lost. I think these are the things that were taken."

Das turned and took the bag, opening it as he stood in the middle of the mess. His eyes widened when he saw the contents. "You just saved my neck! I can't thank you enough."

"You might want to get them to take my prints so they can isolate mine from the robber's. Sorry I couldn't have been more help, but you understand." Evans shrugged. To have done more would have blown his cover. He knew Das would have done the same. "We do have pictures, though. Fairly detailed ones."

Evans signaled Finley over. She began to run through the frames that she had taken of the scene, including those from outside.

"Are you a police photographer?" Das asked, incredulous at his turn of luck. He remembered Finley from the interview he had conducted with her and her sister but didn't recall seeing any indication in the information he had collected of her connection with the police, besides Evans's suggestion that they be read into the case background. That still struck him as highly irregular.

"Nope, just worked with this guy enough to know what you might need to make a case." She nodded at Evans. "If you don't need me here, I'll head back to the room and put these on a thumb drive for you."

Das nodded and Evans followed Finley as she walked to the door. "I will go with her and pick it up. Oh, and by the way, if Mrs. Ruiter wakes up asking for me, tell her I was never here! Thanks!"

The staff had been trying to steer the exiting polo spectators who weren't guests toward the other side of the parade grounds so that they wouldn't see the several police cars that were again in front of the grand entrance to the hotel. For guests, there was no other option. As a result, Logan, Hema, and her parents were standing on the center terrace, asking staff and anyone who passed by what was happening. When Logan saw Finley and Evans, he stepped forward.

"Meadows! Finley! Do you know what's going on?"

Evans responded to his pseudonym and walked over to meet Logan. "Looks like someone tried to rob Sandra. They attacked her, but she's okay. The doctor gave her a sedative."

Logan gasped at the account of Sandra's assault. "I walked her to her room a couple of hours ago. She had a headache from the sun and wanted to sleep it off. I should have stayed with her."

Finley joined the conversation. "I don't think it would have mattered. They would have just come back at another time. I don't think it was a random robbery."

Evans and Logan both turned sharply to look at her. Evans spoke first. "What makes you say that?"

Finley opened her mouth to speak and then remembered that Logan knew Evans only as Meadows. She needed to be sure that she intrigued Evans enough to pursue her hunch, even as she minimized it to Logan.

"Oh, I don't know. It just seemed too well planned. But that's just me meddling." She redirected the conversation back to Logan. "You had better let Hema and her folks know that it's all taken care of and that they're safe." She winked at Logan. "You don't want them packing up and leaving just yet."

She and Evans headed to her room. She pulled out her computer, attached the cable to her camera, and began scrolling through the frames. Evans caught her hand as she passed the shots of Ravi and the man talking at the polo field.

"Who is that?" He was pointing to Ravi. "What's he doing with Ramesh Banerjee?"

Finley gave him Ravi's name and some background on him, from what she knew. "Who is Ramesh Banerjee?"

"One of the most notorious white-collar operators here on the subcontinent. You name it, he can fence it."

"Interesting. Ravi was talking to another guy earlier when we went to Jal Mahal. He had the same body build but with a beard. I don't know if the two incidents are related." Finley let the possible connection percolate awhile. "I would have to search to find those photos."

Evans moved in closer as she began scrolling through the pictures on the compact camera. He stood beside her, his hand on the back of her chair. As shots of interest came on the screen, he leaned in to see the detail. When Max, Whitt, and David came in, they didn't hear the door unlock.

"What's going on?" The ambiguity of Max's question hung in the air as he took in the scene with Evans and Finley. Evans straightened up and turned to the group.

"Mrs. Ruiter was attacked earlier today. Finley interrupted the attack. We are looking for evidence that might lead us to the perpetrators."

Max's eyes narrowed, even as his lip curled slightly. "And you think Finley has the evidence?"

Evans realized where Max's mind was going. He stepped away from the desk, while Finley continued to work. *Glad that she isn't trying to engage him with a denial. He has locked onto this betrayal thing and he isn't letting go. If not Logan, then me. Keep working, Finley, ignore him and it will blow ever. Don't engage him or it will get ugly.*

Finley continued downloading the pictures. When she was finished, she looked up, pure defiance in her eyes. She held up the thumb drive.

"Here you go. I think that's all that Das needs," she said, as he took the drive from her. "When I find the other shots, I'll let you know."

"Thanks. And get some rest. You've had quite a day." He bent down and kissed her forehead before heading for the door. He nodded at David and Whitt as he passed. When he reached Max, he paused and stared, before walking out of the door.

"Finley, are you all right?" Whitt wrapped her arms around her sister. "You look exhausted."

"I'm okay." Finley tried to add some levity to a grim situation. "Death or near death just takes it out of you."

"When did this happen? When did you leave the match?" David asked.

"I headed back during the interval. I heard Sandra cry out as I was passing through the arch, heading to the room. I went to her room and found her on the floor. The guys had run off, but they dropped the bag with the stuff they had stolen. Evans returned it to the police."

"How convenient," Max mumbled. Whitt shot him a murderous glance but bit her tongue.

"Why don't you guys go grab a drink or something while I look after Finley?" Whitt said. "She needs a relaxing bath and a few fingers, neat."

"Good idea," David said, catching Max's shoulder and leading him out of the room. "Get some rest, Finley. Maybe we'll see you at dinner."

David strode purposefully toward the bar. It was early evening, so he and Max had the place to themselves. Max ordered his single malt and David a beer. David wasted no time getting to the point. He had seen for himself Max's reaction to innocuous situations that only became compromising because of his mindset. As soon as the waiter poured his beer, he began.

"Look, Max—"

Max tried to cut him off, but David persisted.

"No, Max, you need to listen. You and Finley need to talk, and you really need to listen this time. Treating her like a pariah isn't going to solve anything." David's frustration was evident in his flushed face. He spoke quickly and decisively, all California languidness gone.

He continued, "If you really believe that she's cheating on you with Logan, or Evans, or both—and, for the record, I do not—then you need to make this relationship right or let her go. Whatever is happening now isn't good, for either of you!"

Max was silent for several minutes, staring into his drink without taking a sip. David feared that he would get up and walk out.

"I don't know what to say to her to make her understand," Max finally muttered.

"If you stop playing games and just say it, I think she'll hear you out. She's confused. I would be, too. But she loves you. That should be enough."

13

IT WAS WELL AFTER MIDNIGHT when Max came back to the room. He and David had continued their conversation until Whitt came down an hour or so later. Finley had drifted off to sleep after a long soak and a good three fingers of bourbon. She was mentally and emotionally wrung out. She had ranted and cried and questioned herself into exhaustion. Whitt had finally slipped out to let her rest. *She'll be good in the morning. Hope Max comes to his senses before then, or that girl will be gone. And I don't think she's coming back. Finley and Evans? What was Max thinking?*

Whitt wandered into the Polo Bar and found the two men talking quietly. She slipped into a seat near David and ordered a glass of chenin blanc. Max had arched an eyebrow at the order, but she was feeling like wine more than champagne right now. Something to soothe rather than excite. They had dragged Max to dinner for fear of what more hours of drinking would do to his liver.

Surprisingly, he was an engaging dinner partner. If he was faking it, he did a good job. He asked about Whitt's conversation with the Indian Central Bank and how microfinance in India differed from what she had seen in Georgia. He quizzed David on promising Georgian and Moldovan wines that he should add to his collection. It was only as the evening grew to an end that the sadness crept back into his voice. Whitt noticed that they had all carefully avoided any conversation of the upcoming wedding. The only acknowledgement was at the end of dinner. Max graciously paid for their meal in celebration of their engagement. When they left him, he was headed back toward the bar.

Max sat with another glass of red wine and thought of what he might say to set it right. He was scared. Scared of saying the wrong thing, scared of facing his demons, but most of all, scared of losing her. If he didn't face the demons and explain it to her, he knew he would lose her for good. If he hadn't already.

After second glass of red, he made his way down the corridor to their room. He quietly opened the door and stood listening for her. She had left a light on for him, as she always did. He went to her side of the bed and stood watching her sleep.

Her hair was a mass of beautiful, chocolate curls that covered most of her pillow. His mother had also had dark tresses that burnished in the sunlight. He knelt beside her and followed the rise and fall of her breath. He saw her tear-streaked face and the damp blotches on her pillow. A tear slipped past him and traveled down his cheek. He had caused her brokenness. He, and only he.

He gently moved a tiny tendril that had fallen across her forehead and watched as she brushed where he had touched with her hand, still deep in sleep. He so wanted to hold her, to kiss her. But he feared that unless he could make her understand, she would pull away from him, widening the already massive chasm that had sought to divide them.

After a time, he sat on the floor beside her, his back against the bedframe. He thought of all the times he had sat in the same position beside his mother's bed as she, too, shed tears over life's hurts and disappointments. Was that what he had become? A disappointment? He prayed not.

Finley stirred in her sleep, turning slowly onto her side. Her hand fell over the edge of the bed, brushing his curls. He leaned over and softly kissed the inside of her wrist. He held his lips there, feeling the tiniest rhythm of her pulse.

She stirred again, this time half opening her eyes. She squinted Max into focus and then drew a sharp breath. She held it until he touched her cheek, first with his finger and then with his lips.

She exhaled and then took in the full scent of him. The sandalwood and bergamot of his cologne, the richness of his wined breath, the cleanness of his skin. She closed her eyes and waited.

"Sorry. I didn't mean to wake you." He swallowed hard. "I just needed to touch you."

She remained silent. She needed to listen, not speak.

"I'm going to learn from David and put it out there. Stop rationalizing and try instead to communicate with you. You, of all people, know I'm not good at that. But I'll try."

Finley opened her eyes slowly and looked at him. His head was down, as if in prayer. She waited, listening to his breathing as he collected his thoughts.

After several minutes, he continued. "I let my insecurities get out of hand—Whitt and David's wedding and the whole question of marriage. Logan and my jealousy. I tried to sort through them all, so I could explain them to you. So I could help you understand. All it did was drive me crazy, because even I couldn't make sense of them. I acted out instead, and that pushed you away. Fin, I'm so sorry. Please forgive me. I love you so much it scares me."

She reached out and ran her fingers through his dark curls. He brought his beautiful eyes even with hers and smiled. He took her hand and kissed each of her fingers in turn.

"Max, help me understand. I'm listening," she said softly, and she waited the several minutes until he spoke again.

"When I was about eleven, my life imploded. My mother must have found out that my father was cheating and decided to pay him back with a string of men of her own. I couldn't understand how my loving parents had turned on each other. I was caught in the middle."

"Why didn't they divorce?"

"They did, eventually, when I was thirteen. But the damage was done. The arguments, the accusations. Marriage as an institution got tainted. Not rational, but it is what it is."

Finley had pulled herself into a sitting position as he spoke. She watched the strong, in-control man she had always known turn into a scared, young boy. *Maybe the control is a defense so that he never has to go through that again. I know defenses.*

She thought back on the few times he had talked about his family. Except for the mention that he was from Old Saybrook, Connecticut, she knew very little. She recalled that his parents were still alive but were divorced. He was close to his mother but only saw her periodically because of both of their travel schedules, or so they said. She wondered now whether there might be more to it. Unlike her crazy clan, his was not a particularly large or close family.

Max turned to look up at her. "When I see you with Logan or Evans, I make all sorts of stupid associations, so what's innocent becomes sordid. I know I need to work through that. Hell, when both your supposed rivals tell you you've got a problem of perception, you *may* have a little problem," he laughed raggedly. "I'm trying. But it may take more time than you'll give me. Will you give me a chance to sort it out, make it right?" His voice was barely above a whisper.

Finley's voice caught in her throat. She waited, carefully weighing her words and their possible impact before she spoke.

"Max, I hope you know that I love you. But to be honest, I'm in self-protection mode right now. I have to be. I'm too emotionally fragile to go through this again." Finley's voice grew stronger as she spoke. She knew it had to be said. "So, you tell me, which is it? If you don't want to be with me, have the balls enough to say so. I'll go, but you can't keep drawing me close just to push me away again. Just say it, and I will never grace your door again."

Max had gotten up from the floor to sit on the edge of the bed, staring at his hands. His brow had furrowed, and his breath had quickened. It was now or never. He had to make her see or he would lose her.

Sadness, defeat, and confusion claimed his face, his shoulders, his bearing. Finley wanted to reassure him, but the need to help him make it right was overpowered by anger and frustration at the patterns of their relationship that kept them rotating in a downward spiral. She said nothing. She waited.

"I know I'm asking a lot. I have hurt you so many times, so deeply. I'm afraid of hurting you again if I can't work this out. The truth is you want marriage, and I may never be able to give it to you." He drew in a deep breath. His jaw flexed before relaxing as he continued, "I suspect my fear of marriage is all tied up with my parents. That's part of the reason I didn't ask you in Casablanca. I had never thought about marriage until you. Then I had all these conflicting thoughts, and I never asked when I should have."

He kept staring at his hands as he spoke. "Whitt and David's engagement brought it all back. I knew marriage, us, was going to come up and I couldn't talk about it. I may never be comfortable with marriage. Part of me says I should be like Evans and bow out so maybe you could find happiness with someone like Logan. He loves you. They both do, far more maturely than I have."

"I love you, but if I'm honest, truly honest, I don't want to get married. Not now. Maybe not ever. I want permanence but not marriage. Maybe the best way to prove that I do love you is to let you go, so you can marry, since that's what you want." Max blew out a long breath. He was struggling with the desire to keep her close even while he knew he may need to set her free.

Finley was now sitting on her heels. She had listened long enough. She pulled herself to her knees, her hands on her hips. She was angry now and decided to speak her mind.

"Who said I needed marriage? You just assumed," she said. "You assumed I'd choose partnership at the firm over being with you and so you never asked me to stay. And now you assume that the only options are marriage or us splitting." She swung her legs over the edge of the bed and stood over him. "You keep making assumptions. And where has that gotten us?"

She took his hands in hers and implored him, "Stop making decisions for me. Love me, honor me, trust me enough to make the right ones for myself. I don't need marriage. I need a commitment from you. Something, in all this push and pull, you have never once given me."

Max looked at her, absolutely baffled. He was quiet as he processed what she had just said.

"That's all you need? My commitment? My love ever after? You're sure about no marriage? Even if we have kids?"

"Even if we have kids. If you say you're mine, then I'm yours! That simple!"

Max let the tears of relief flow. The years of holding it all together came undone. The years of pushing her away before she could go away were over. The years of fearing he would disappoint her were in the past.

"That simple?"

"Max, love doesn't have to be hard. It was designed to be really simple. We make it hard."

She climbed into his lap, wiping his face with the end of her T-shirt. "Baby, please talk to me. Always. I don't know what I'm supposed to do when you shut me out. If in doubt, say it out loud from now on!"

He buried his head in her hair and breathed her in. "Always!"

They continued their conversation well into the morning. Finley had heard his explanation of the surface hurts that had left him tentative in so many ways. What she needed now, if she were to let down her defenses, was to understand what lay beneath the surface, where his real tender points were. She needed to be aware of them so that, if she had to probe them to keep their relationship on track, she knew where he was most vulnerable, where she needed to tread carefully.

She also wanted him to hear her pain points, where she had grown callouses in order to get through life. She shared with him mistakes she had made in her marriage to Grant. Her tendency to appease, for example, rather than stating her preferences.

"I never would have guessed," Max said, as she lay in his arms, his hand stroking her hair. "You always seem so clear in what you want, where you are going. It's hard to see that as anyone's decision but yours."

Finley chortled. "I'm glad I have the world convinced! Most of the time, I am second-guessing myself like nobody's business. I go along to get along. It's only when I'm pushed too far off course that I push back. And sometimes it's too late to get back on track."

"Is that what happened to you and Grant?" Max asked.

"Yeah. I guess I wanted to be with him so badly that I didn't really listen to what he was saying." Finley nodded. "Or maybe he didn't say all he was thinking for fear I wouldn't agree. Whatever it was, we ended up on parallel tracks going in different directions."

She paused and then murmured, "I don't want that to happen to us."

"It won't . . . I know it almost did. Twice. But I hope we have learned our lessons. I know I have. And if I forget, please remind me. There is too much at stake for us to remain silent." Max looked at her and whispered, "I can't go through life with a broken heart. And not having you would break it. Irreparably."

"As it would for me." Finley reached up to touch the light stubble that was growing on his chin. "I will remind you if you promise to do the same for me."

"Promi—" He was interrupted by her kiss, which grew in intensity until he found himself unable to breathe. The thought of life without her had been unbearable. The thought of life with her was all he wanted to focus on now. *She says she's mine. I have always been hers. Now to prove it to her.*

14

WHITT AND DAVID WERE ALREADY halfway through breakfast when Finley and Max found their way to the table. They had slept in, exhausted from their late-night conversation. The murder of Elise and the attack on Sandra added another layer of emotion that weighed on Finley.

"Finally, you're up. I was getting ready to call security and have them check on you." Whitt smiled wryly as she took in the pair.

Max had helped Finley get seated and ordered her coffee. All good signs from what Whitt could tell. But Finley could be a sly one, letting him think all was well until she called the car to take her to the airport, leaving him behind. It was hard to say.

"Did you sleep well?" Finley asked her sister and future brother-in-law. She had an idea what Whitt's side-glances were looking for. She decided she wasn't going to make it easy for her sister to tell whether she and Max were on again or off again.

"Yes, we were out like a light after dinner," David said. "How late did you stay up after we left, Max?"

"It was around midnight when I left."

Max was pensive this morning. He had laid out his soul last night and today was feeling exposed. He glanced at Finley and caught her gazing at him. He wondered what she thought of the man beside her. So cold—cruel even—a few days before and yet so vulnerable last night. *She must think I have lost my mind. I suspect I have. Maybe she can help me find it.*

"What's the plan for today?" Finley shifted her glance between David and Whitt. She figured Max was like her—too depleted to make any voluntary decisions.

"We had thought of going to the Anokhi Museum," David volunteered. "They have a block printing operation there that's supposed to be fun. We amateurs get to try to print like the masters."

"We're trying to keep it light with all the investigations going on," Whitt added. "Have you heard any more from Evans?"

She hesitated to bring up his name, given Max's potential reaction, but she wanted to know. David had recounted some of his conversation with Max, so she had some understanding of Max's sensitivities. However, the reality was that there were two murders and an attack that were still unsolved. She suspected that the police, and the hotel, were treating Ajai's death as a closed case, whatever cause of death they had assigned to it.

That left Elise's death and Sandra's mugging to unravel. She had little confidence in the local police to figure out what happened. Not because they couldn't, but because they were disinclined to probe too deeply. They would likely find someone plausible to pin it on, pat themselves on the back for quickly solving the case, and move on.

"No. Nothing after I gave him the photos for Inspector Das," Finley said. "That reminds me. I need to go through the other frames and find the pictures that Evans's wanted of the man Ravi was talking to."

"The guy that you showed me yesterday?" Whitt asked.

Finley nodded. If both the man Evans had pointed out at the polo match and the man that Finley had seen on the dock, and again at the jewelry store, were involved in the jewelry fraud operation,

Ravi was in trouble. She wondered how deep into this Ravi was. He didn't seem like a bad person, but then, Ted Bundy looked like the boy next door. Whatever his involvement, he needed to watch his step. Evans had confirmed that Banerjee didn't settle scores with a tap on the hand.

"Why do you think Sandra was attacked?" Max joined the conversation now that he had some coffee and food in him.

"I don't know. As I told Evans, I don't think that it was a random robbery gone wrong. I think she was targeted," Finley opined. "Things must have gone wrong when she came back to her room early."

"Which means that they may have others on the list of targets," Whitt concluded.

"More troubling to me is that because the stash that they took from Sandra was recovered, they are most likely going to need to make up the shortfall somehow. To the people behind this, this is a business," Finley suggested.

"Who of the guests has the most jewelry?" Max cast an eye on Whitt. "They can't hit Sandra again, so who is next?"

"Don't look at me," she laughed. "I may collect a lot, but they aren't high quality or high worth. If they are, I put them in the front desk vault. That's where I think they'll hit."

"I think you're right. I did notice a lot more police coverage in and around the building," Max noted.

"I would also hope that they have warned guests of the need to secure their jewelry now," Finley said. "I know Hema and her mother as well as Devya and others have brought jewelry with them to wear at dinner. I've seen some of it. It's exquisite and probably worth a lot."

"You raise a good point," Max said. "Does anyone know what happened to Elise's jewelry after she died?"

"Yes, especially that gorgeous cabochon ruby she always wore." Whitt sounded covetous of that piece.

"I would guess that the police have all of that in custody," David surmised.

"One would hope," Finley mused.

She looked up as Evans approached the table, his brow furrowed. He greeted the group, making a point to stand away from Finley to avoid comment from Max.

"Can we offer you a cup of coffee?" Max pointed to a chair, much to the surprise of the others. "You look like you have the weight of the world on your shoulders right now."

"I guess it would be more in keeping with my cover, but frankly, I don't really care." Evans sat and thanked the waiter for the cup he brought, unsolicited. He poured himself a cup and then held the pot up to the others. They all declined. He continued to scan the terrace and surrounding area, his hawklike intensity increasing.

"What's up?" David asked. "You look like you're looking for something. Was there another robbery?"

"No more robberies, thank goodness, but we do have a missing person." Evans returned to surveying the grounds.

"Who?" Whitt was scanning the area, trying to think of who was missing. Until an hour ago, she would have started her list with Max and Finley.

"Ravi Malhotra." Evans lowered his voice. "His wife reported him missing to the hotel security this morning. She said he didn't come to the room last night."

"Did they argue?" Finley asked. "He may have gone somewhere to cool off."

Evans smiled. "We thought of that, but she says that they hadn't. In fact, they'd had a nice dinner together in the restaurant last night before she headed to the room and he to the bar."

"That's odd. We were in the restaurant, or had a view of it, for much of the evening after the polo match, almost until they closed. I don't recall seeing either of them." David turned to Max and Whitt for confirmation. They both nodded. "Did the barman see him?"

"I don't know whether Das checked. I will have to ask." Evans shook his head slowly. "That is strange. Why would she lie? This is making less and less sense."

"Where have you looked thus far?" Max asked. "This is a sizeable property. Maybe he wandered somewhere to sleep off a bender."

"The police brought in a search team with dogs a couple hours ago. We are combing the grounds now."

"Did you also check the empty rooms?" Finley suggested. "He may have gone into one to sleep it off."

Evan stood and drained the last of his coffee. "Thanks for this—and the suggestions. Enjoy what's left of your stay. And stay out of trouble!"

He directed his last comment to Whitt and Finley. In the several times that he had encountered the sisters, whether in Morocco, Sri Lanka, or here in India, they had managed to get themselves into some hair-raising situations. He or his team had managed to extricate them each time, but sometimes just barely.

"Where do you think Ravi has gotten himself to?" Finley asked after Evans had left. "Something's up."

"And I'll bet Devya knows more than she is saying," Whitt added, raising an eyebrow to Finley. She hesitated before continuing. "Do you think Logan knows anything?"

Finley paused and then shrugged. "I saw him with Hema last, so he may not have been with Ravi and Devya at all last night. Who knows?"

"May I suggest that we leave the sleuthing to the police and find an activity to divert us?" Max proposed. "You had mentioned the Anokhi Museum."

"We did." David looked at his watch. "It's out near Amber Fort, so we can make a day of it—or what's left of the day. You guys game?"

Max turned to Finley. "What do you think?"

"Works for me," Finley said. "Can you give me thirty minutes or so find the pictures for Evans, and then we can go? I'll drop the stick at the front desk, and he can pick it up later."

In the room, Finley pulled out her computer and found another thumb drive for Evans. She was going to have to ask Das to give her drives back after the police finished downloading the evidence. She would have none left when she headed back to the field.

She connected her camera and used her monitor to get a better view of the faces on each frame. While she knew to include the sequence at the dock, she took her time studying frames in which there were people, in case she missed other times in which either the bearded man or his clean-shaven counterpart showed up. She found three frames in which a man resembling Banerjee showed up. She would leave it to Evans and Das to confirm the identity.

"I'm ready to go."

Max looked up from his *International Herald Tribune* and smiled. "Then grab the rest of your camera stuff and let's go before you think of something else you need to do."

She gave him a playful tap for his flippant comment, followed by a peck on his lips. Max, unsatisfied by the brevity of the kiss, took her in his arms and kissed her fully.

"Let's not ever do that again." Max looked down at her and planted another kiss on her forehead.

"What? Kiss like that?" Finley teased. "Pity. I rather liked it."

"You! No, argue like we did. I know it is on me to do better at telling you what scares me. But I was so afraid of losing you again. I can't tell you how scared I was."

Finley was silent. At some point, she would explain how close he came to doing just that, but right now she decided on a different tack.

"Just keep talking to me. I may not always understand, but I will always try to listen with an open heart. If you offer me the same courtesy, I think we'll be okay."

She kissed him lightly again and grabbed her satchel. They were almost at the lobby when Finley reached in her bag for her fan.

"Darn, I forgot my fan!" Finley sighed. "Why don't you go ahead? I know David and Whitt are probably wondering where we are. I'll just run back and get it." She handed him the thumb drive she had in her hand. "And can you drop this off at the desk for Evans?"

"Okay, but hurry it up," Max said, smiling.

Finley retraced her steps back to the room. She pulled her key from her bag as she went. When she got to the door, she inserted the key and pushed the door open. She couldn't remember exactly where she put the fan. She thought it was on the bedside table. In any event, she didn't anticipate that it would take long. As such, she didn't bother to fully close the door.

It was only when she rounded the corner from the sitting room into the bedroom that she realized that she wasn't alone. Two men, both of whom she had seen before but did not know, were standing in the dressing room. For a moment, she thought she could back out of the room before they saw her, so focused was their concentration on searching through her things.

She had just reached the opening when the bearded one looked up. He gave her a twisted smile and a shake of his head.

"That's too bad. You coming back," he said matter-of-factly. "Good for us, but not so good for you. Where is it?"

"What are you talking about?" Finley was more puzzled than frightened.

"The necklace. Don't play dumb!" the other man growled.

When he turned around, she realized it wasn't Ramesh Banerjee, as she had anticipated, but a younger version of him. *What is this, some sort of family business? They all look related—same body build, same facial structure. Some use these observations will be if I don't make it out of here. Stay calm and think.*

"Don't stand there looking dumb. Just give us the necklace."

"I don't have any necklace. What I have is all there. Take it all and sort it later, but you aren't going to find any necklace in that stuff."

"Well, if you don't have it, then your sister must. Maybe we'll just pay her a visit and see whether she has what we are looking for."

Finley knew that Whitt and David were safely waiting for her in the lobby with Max. Going into her sister's room might buy her time. And, as importantly, someone might see her as they moved rooms and go for help. The only problem with the plan was that she didn't have a key for Whitt and David's room.

"Look, do what you want. But I don't have a key to their room!"

"No problem. We do!" The bearded man moved toward her, this time with a knife. "Don't try anything, or this will end very badly for you. And I rather like your pretty face."

He touched her cheek with the back of his hand.

"Soft, too."

"Arun, cut it out. Put the knife away. We are just supposed to get the necklace and get out of here. No more mistakes," the Banerjee look-alike demanded.

The bearded man flinched at the last of the younger man's words. Nonetheless, he folded the knife and stuck it in his pocket. He took a firm grasp of Finley's arm, twisting it sharply behind her, and pulled her into the hall.

"Then let's go. Junior, open the room next door. Maybe we'll have better luck."

In the nanosecond before Junior stepped out of her room, Finley heard the door to Whitt's room click. Her heart dropped. *Whitt or David has come back for something. They'll hurt all of us. Please let someone see us.* Arun tightened the grip on her arm, momentarily throwing her off-balance.

"Don't even think of trying to get away. I can outrun you any day of the week," he whispered loudly in her ear. He smelled of onions and cheap cologne. The combination sickened her. She swallowed the bile that had risen in her throat.

Junior unlocked the door and slowly pushed it open. He stuck his head in to ensure that the room was empty. Finley was confused. She could have sworn that she had heard someone go in. Maybe it was just the wind, pushing the door more closed.

"You are going to sit right here while we go through this room, and then we are going to go through the next one. You had better pray that your dear sissy has the necklace, or things are going to look really bad for you."

"I don't know what you are talking about," Finley repeated. "What necklace?"

"The one from the dead woman!" the bearded man hissed, as the younger man methodically opened all the pockets on both Whitt's and David's computer cases and then went through all the drawers in the desk.

"You two found the body. The dead lady had a big stone on all day, but when the body was recovered, there was no stone. So where did it go?"

Finley wondered how they could have known all this information. Were they watching all the guests or just the ones they targeted? How could they have seen the recovery of the body? The security guard had cordoned off the area from all guests and staff by the time he walked Finley and Whitt back to their rooms. Where—and who—were their lookouts?

"You, up. We're moving into the next room." The bearded man grabbed Finley by the hair this time to get her to her feet. She cried out and twisted toward him, just as Evans stepped from the bedroom, gun drawn.

"I don't think you are going anywhere," Evans said, punching out every word.

Finley could never remember the sequence of the next few seconds. Evans trained the gun on the younger man, even as he watched the bearded man attempt to drag Finley to the door as his hostage. The yank brought her close enough to him for her to bring her heel down on his instep with her full body weight.

The man dropped the wad of hair he had in his hand and released her arm as he grabbed a chair to stabilize himself. Not wanting to be captured, he headed for the door and threw it open, only to be met by Max's fist. He stiffened before falling backward into the room in a comatose heap.

Within seconds, the police arrived to handcuff the men and take them to the station. It took two men to carry the still unconscious bearded man out of the room, while guests looked on.

"Are you all right?" Max scanned Finley for signs of injury.

"I'm fine. Still trying to figure out what just happened." Finley rubbed her scalp gently. "He was pretty strong."

Evans had dropped his gun back into his leg holster and stood leaning against the wall, looking at the two of them.

"I don't think I could have sequenced it better if I were working with seasoned agents." He smiled. "You two want a job?"

"Not on your life." Finley shook her head. "You better tell all your women agents to keep their hair short. Who knew it could be such an effective weapon?"

"Who were those two goons and what were they doing in our room?" Whitt had pushed past the police to reach her sister. She gently touched Finley's cheek, even as Max held her. "What happened? Did they hurt you?"

"Just pulled my hair, but I'll survive." She looked at Evans. "How did you get into this room?"

Evans pointed at Max. "Ask your boyfriend. He's the mastermind here."

"You can tell us all about it—over drinks," Whitt stated, as she led the way to the bar.

WHITT HAD THEM ICE A bottle of Pol Roger, even though only she and her sister were drinking champagne. David had opted for a glass of cabernet, and Max and Evans ordered single malts. When the drinks were poured, Whitt offered a toast.

"To my danger-prone sister and the men who saved her!" Whitt said.

"Hold on. Your sister pretty much saved herself. She was brilliant," Evans interjected. "Max's jab was icing on the cake. All I did was pull a gun!"

Evans recounted for Whitt, David, and Max what had happened once the men had moved Finley to Whitt's room. Finley filled them all in on what had happened in the moments before, when she had entered her room. She was still confused on how Evans and Max knew she needed help.

"Max overheard part of the conversation through the crack in the door and came looking for me," Evans relayed.

"I saw Evans on the terrace and told him that you were in trouble," Max explained. "I remembered the connecting door between our two suites and thought he might be able to enter through Whitt's room."

"I showed my credentials and got the maid to open the room. Max went to call security and the police," Evans recounted. "I got in just as you switched rooms."

"What were they looking for anyway?" David asked.

"Elise's necklace. They got it in their head that between the time that she died and the time that she was taken away in the ambulance, the necklace was taken," Finley said. "Since we found the body, they assumed that we had the necklace."

"How did they know that the necklace wasn't on the body when it was taken away?" Whitt wondered.

"That's what I want to know. I think these guys have lookouts or moles working in the hotel." Finley rubbed her head again. It was starting to tingle. She found a pain reliever in her bag and took it. She looked up to find Max observing her with a frown. She reached for his hand to reassure him.

"That is something we need to figure out—and fast. If they have someone inside, then everything we do is exposed to Banerjee." Evans looked worried. "And now that my cover is blown, we may be more vulnerable than ever."

He looked at Finley and Max as he finished his drink and stood to leave. "If you two want jobs, the offer is still open. I need to see what we can get out of the suspects we brought in. I need to figure out how to shut down Banerjee's operations—and quickly."

He placed his hand on Finley's shoulder. "Take care of that head. We'll be back tonight to get your statements."

Whitt poured more champagne into her sister's glass. "Well, to my danger-prone sister who can take care of herself, then! Are we hanging here or heading out? I am fine either way."

Max looked at Finley with concern. "How's your head? You've had quite a day!"

"I'm fine. I say, let's go to Anokhi," Finley replied. "I'll deal with the mess in our room later. I want to see the museum."

The Anokhi Museum was housed in an ornately decorated, sixteenth-century, earthen-pink mansion, reminiscent of the Hawa Mahal. After touring the skillfully curated museum, the Four Musketeers tried their hand at block printing. Large, square blocks of wood were intricately cut into repeating patterns that were inked in an array of natural pink, red, blue, and green dyes. They were then transferred to a sheet of thin cotton. The masters were able to ink bolts of richly patterned material without anyone being able to tell where one block ended and another started.

As much as they tried, all four of them failed at pattern alignment. The print master laughed heartily at their end products, allowing them to take the cotton scraps with them, since they were of no use to him.

The highlight of their afternoon, however, was Finley's shopping spree, a rarity for her. She purchased five intricately blocked kurtas in her favorite blues and greens in record speed.

"You bought as much as I did. And so fast. No hesitation or pondering. I could never do that," Whitt remarked. "Had I known you liked these things this much, I would have been gifting them to you long ago."

"I didn't know they were so comfortable until I got a couple in Ranchi to wear to the site," Finley said. "They breathe, so it is not so hot working under the sun. And they are roomy, so I can move."

They settled into the small café in the museum's center courtyard for a late lunch. All their senses were piqued in that tiny space. The pink of the building contrasted with the sharp blue of the sky. Lemon and orange trees in bright-blue, earthen pots lined the perimeter, complementing the visual color scheme. The aroma of grilled meats and vegetables wafted into every corner of the space, carried by a constant cross breeze that cut through the square.

The foursome turned to investigate every time a new dish was brought out. When their orders of curry pies and masala-spiced chicken were finally placed, they returned to the events of the day.

"You may have cornered some jewel thieves, but it doesn't answer all the questions I have." Whitt was picking at pieces of *papadam* as she spoke. "The one that is most pressing is where is Ravi?"

"That is a significant, open question," Finley added. "If it were an argument or a bender, he would have surfaced by now, I would think."

"Do you think those men killed him and buried his body somewhere?" Whitt's clear-green eyes grew large as she considered the possibility.

"I wouldn't have put it past those two, but I didn't see any residual blood on the knife when he held it up," Finley recalled.

Max was incredulous. "My God, woman, you had the presence of mind to check the blade to see if it was clean?"

"If it had been Whitt or Mama, they would have offered him a wet wipe!" Finley laughed. "Look, those guys were not above killing, but I don't think they killed Ravi. I think he's some place on the grounds. I also think he's involved."

"Really? How?" David asked, as he tucked into a curry pie.

"That is what I don't know," Finley answered.

"Do you think he's the lookout?" Max asked.

"I'm having a hard time placing him in locations where things happened. For example, when Sandra was attacked, he was on the polo field, I'm almost sure."

"You have a point. But that's the type of analysis that needs to be done to figure out his role," Max advised.

"Or you could just find him and ask him," Finley added.

Whitt said what everyone was hoping. "Maybe Evans will have found him by the time we get back."

The sun was a large, orange ball in a dusty sky when the car pulled into the Rambaugh driveway some two hours later. The doorman welcomed them and told them that Mr. Meadows was waiting for them in the Polo Bar.

"Did you have a nice outing?" Evans, aka Meadows, asked. He was reclining in one of the leather barrel chairs, drink in hand. Finley knew from experience it was most likely a single malt. Das sat beside him, less relaxed but not as rigidly businesslike as she would have expected. *They must have broken the case. Das would never be this laid-back unless the pressure was off.*

"We did indeed. We all should stick to our day jobs, but trying the block printing was informative. I learned never to let David hang curtains or shelves without a level," Whitt joked. She communicated in unspoken code to Finley, and a bottle of Pol Roger was placed on ice to chill.

"What about you? Was it a productive afternoon?" Finley was dying to find out the details. She knew they had come to take their statements, but she hoped that she could get more information than she gave.

"It has indeed. We found Ravi—in one of the empty suites. Thanks for the idea. It may have taken us a while to have gotten to that one." Evans smiled at Finley.

"Why was he in an empty room?" Max asked. "Was he hiding from someone?"

"He should have been. But it was too late for that." Evans shook his head at some fact that he knew but had yet to be surfaced for the rest of the assembled group.

Max leaned forward slightly to catch Evans's eye, his face dark. "Too late? He's okay, isn't he?"

"He's alive. Beat up pretty badly, but nothing life-threatening," Evans conveyed. "I'll let Das fill you in."

Inspector Das was, by now, getting used to the fact that these guests were regularly brought in, unofficially, on official police matters. While highly irregular in his experience, he had to admit that it had proven effective in this case and probably led to faster resolution of what turned out to be a tangled web of intrigue.

"After the two men who entered your rooms were taken to the station, we began a room-to-room search of the hotel in cooperation with the hotel management. We started, per your suggestion, with the empty rooms, and those farthest from reception first. We were acting on the supposition you had put forth that he was likely to be found as far away from other guests as possible," Das relayed.

He took a sip of his ginger ale and continued, "We had only opened three of the rooms before we found him. He was bound and gagged, and, as Chief Inspector Evans said, had been beaten about the face and body."

"We got him medical attention, and he started asking about the other two men. That is when we suspected that he was deeply involved in this venture. It turns out that they had turned on him when he got cold feet and refused to complete the assignment," Evans added.

"What was the assignment?" Max asked. "How do all these pieces—this robbery, the attack on Sandra, and Elise's murder—fit together?"

"Don't forget the boy's death," Evans added.

"So, they were responsible for Ajai as well?" Finley was beginning to realize how much danger she had been in with the two burglars. They would likely have killed her if they hadn't found the necklace. Where was the necklace, anyway? Had the police recovered it? She would ask after the murders had been explained.

"Yes. The kid was just collateral damage. Apparently, one of the inside guys—and we still aren't sure who all of them are—had put something in one of the target's drinks. We think it was Sandra's. Somehow it was spilled, not drunk, and the houseboy was sent to clean it up. He must have taken a sip. It would have been fine if he hadn't had an allergic reaction to the sedative."

"That was why you couldn't match the sedative when you did the med search. It had been brought in from outside." Finley was ticking off the questions that were being answered. There still were a lot more that needed resolution.

"The boy's death was accidental, but because it happened as part of the commission of a crime, it is likely that they will be charged for it." Das glanced at Evans to see if he wanted to pick up the story. Evans shook his head and let Das resume the tale.

"It appears that Mrs. Boyd-Hampton was killed because of something she overheard," Das reported.

"This is Ravi's account of the events, since the other two are as mum as the tomb," Evans added. "Heaven only knows how accurate it is, but it gives us something to go on. I beg your pardon, Das, please continue."

"Yes, as was said, Mr. Malhotra has suggested that Mrs. Boyd-Hampton heard something, or at least was seen listening to a conversation, about the boy or another heist, and she was killed to keep her quiet. We know the cause of death was poison, viper venom in her thermos, but we don't know when it was put there or by whom."

"That is why figuring out who the other inside men are is crucial to this case. For all we know, they may have disappeared by now," Evans concluded.

"Can't you check the hotel for any dismissals or other terminations in the last few days?" David asked.

Max took a sip of his drink. "That assumes that they came in under the cover of hired staff. They may have just slipped in and out dressed as staff without formally being part of staff."

"In that case, you have to interview pretty much all of the staff to see who they remember being around that was new or unfamiliar," Finley interjected. "But that is going to be hard, since you don't want to tip them off."

Das glanced at Evans and smiled. "Now I see why you bring them into your cases!"

"So, we have an explanation for Ajai's death and a partial answer for Elise's. But why was Sandra attacked? Was it just bad timing?" Whitt asked.

Das nodded. "I think the burglars thought the room was empty and that they had time to go through and switch out the jewels they were to take. Their modus was not to ransack but rather to go in, take the original piece, and substitute it for a high-quality paste job."

"Now this is getting interesting." Whitt stared at Finley until she caught on to the connection that Whitt was making between the real stones, the man in the jewelry store, and getting the stolen goods out of the country. "Finley, why don't you share your idea?"

Evans and Das turned to look at Finley, who shrugged. "It's crazy. I'll tell them later."

"Why don't you tell us now?" Evans's voice was measured, his tone firm.

"The guy who I saw Ravi with at the dock was in the jewelry store in the arcade," Finley began.

"The one here in the hotel?" Evans let out a low whistle when she nodded.

"Tell him the rest!" Whitt prodded.

"I'm just surmising. I mean, what if the syndicate uses arrangements with legitimate jewelry businesses to transport the stones out of the country?" Finley hypothesized. "Let's say I buy a necklace in the shop here and then want it shipped to the States, these guys will ship it. So the syndicate, acting as the shipping company, sends paste to the customer, pops out the real stones, and mixes them with some other stolen stones before shipping them to a fictitious buyer, who is their courier, using the jeweler's credentials."

Whitt jumped in. "Then, if customs or the police check, there is an invoice for a shipment of jewelry with the right paperwork that corresponds. Everything would look in order, even though it isn't."

"As I said, it's crazy," Finley said quietly, staring at the bubbles in her champagne.

"The theory is ragged in places, but you might just be on to something." Evans smiled to himself. "How do you come up with these things?"

"She's worse than I am," Finley laughed, pointing at her sister. "But sometimes the craziest schemes end up holding water."

"All right, so we have your syndicate head and his boys stealing stones and shipping them out—and killing anyone who gets in their way," David mused. "But where does Ravi come in?"

"Ah, yes, Ravi. Your dear friend." Evans smiled.

"He's a friend of a friend," Whitt was quick to say. "We just met him this weekend!"

"Das, you want to explain?" Evans asked.

"Apparently, Ravi is the procurer. He finds targets, befriends them, takes pictures with them, and then passes the pictures to his contact at the syndicate so that the fakes can be made," Das explained.

He continued, "Once he has the paste replicas, if he can do it without arousing suspicion, he replaces the fake for the real piece, or he provides his contact with the target's schedule, routine, and habits so they can take care of the switch."

"I don't think Ravi knew when he got into this that people were going to be killed," Evans conjectured. "That's why they sidelined him until they could figure out what to do with him. He backed out of helping to search for the necklace in your room."

"Does Logan know?" Finley asked. She was saddened that her friend had been taken in.

Evans nodded. "We sent a team with him to have the plane checked out. I wouldn't be surprised if they find a few caches of jewels hidden in the most unusual places."

"How's Devya taking all of this?" Whitt's mouth twisted like she had sucked in lemon juice at the mention of the woman's name.

"She followed him into the lobby, yelling and screaming about how her parents had told her he was just a 'jumped-up desk jockey,' in her words." Evans tried to stifle a laugh. "It was quite a scene."

Das was equally amused. "She has refused to post his bail so he will have to stay in the cells tonight."

Finley imagined Ravi in his designer shoes and bespoke shirts sitting in a crowded Indian jail cell. She caught a mental whiff of the smells and turned up her nose in disgust.

"We wanted to let you know where we were in the case and thank you for all your help." Evans shifted his gaze to rest squarely on Finley and Whitt. "However, you two need to take separate vacations, henceforth. Together, you are dangerous."

Finley and Whitt had to laugh. It was true. Murder seemed to fall into their laps.

"An officer will be here in a bit to take formal statements," Das said. "We need to try to tie up the last loose ends so we can close this case out."

"Do you happen to know how we can find out information about Ajai's family?" Finley asked. "We would like to send them something."

"I will have the officer bring it when he comes to take your statements." Das pushed his chair back and stood. "Again, my thanks."

When Evans and Das had left, the Four Musketeers settled back into their drinks.

"What do you want to do for dinner?" David asked, predictably. They all broke into laughter.

16

DINNER FELT LIKE OLD TIMES. David and Whitt kept them in stitches with their contrasting views of David's engagement speech. Whitt recalled that he had asked her to spend the rest of her days with him, travelling the world. David's recollection was that he had asked her to travel the world and spend the rest of her days with him. The difference, while subtle, was important to Whitt, since it had been one of the conditions to her accepting his proposal when he first floated the idea. Whitt wanted to be sure that he understood that travel was always going to be part of the bargain, not just something she did until she settled down.

That girl may marry, but she ain't never settling down, Finley thought with an understanding smile. It must be part of the Montgomery-Blake wanderlust that ran through their veins.

"Check the contract!" was all Finley could say between fits of laughter. She could imagine her sister rifling through her brain to see if she had inadvertently agreed to quitting her job, moving to Tbilisi, and becoming a housewife, or any other circumstance that would curtail her travel. David may have understood it as her need for a few more years of adventure before she settled down, but it was becoming clear that in Whitt's mind, the travel never ended. David would get used to it.

Max watched the exchange with sad amusement. He wondered if Finley would regret not having the same memories of the proposal moment. What else could he give her that would be uniquely theirs? Something that marked the moment when "he" and "she" became "we." She caught him looking at her and returned his glance with a quizzical smile. In response, he mouthed "Love you," and sat back in satisfaction when she whispered, "More."

Logan had found them to tell them about Ravi's turn of events. Devya had left for Delhi on the evening commercial flight, despite his offer of the plane. From the description of the exchange, Logan doubted he would ever see her again in life. He didn't seem particularly upset about that conclusion.

"I am so sorry about all this. Finley, I never would have put you in such danger if I had any idea." Logan took the glass of champagne Whitt offered as he joined the table after dinner. "Ravi always seemed like a stand-up sort of guy. Ambitious, but who isn't? I never would have imagined this."

"Have you seen or spoken with him?" Finley asked.

"Yeah, after Devya dissed him, I went down to the station to post his bail. He's still a friend," Logan said. "I'll probably stick around to be sure that he shows up in court, so I am not carted off to jail in his stead or declared persona non grata in India."

He drained the last of his champagne, refusing Whitt's offer of more. "Since I'm not going anywhere immediately, I'll have the plane take you all back to Delhi. Just let me know what time you want to head out. I'm assuming sometime in the afternoon."

He made the rounds of goodnights, placing a kiss on Finley's forehead last. "Hema and I will see you off tomorrow."

"So, she's sticking around, too?" Finley asked with a smile.

"Yep. We'll see where it goes," Logan chuckled. "Her parents haven't banned me from seeing her yet, even after all this. So that's encouraging."

"I will keep my fingers crossed," Finley murmured. "You deserve good. We both do."

Exhausted from an overly eventful day, the two couples had ambled back to their rooms not long after talking to Logan. While Max showered, Finley pulled out her camera and began to cull her pictures. She had almost finished reviewing the frames on the small camera when several photos caught her eye. She connected her camera to the monitor, enlarged the frame, and scrolled back several shots.

She couldn't remember exactly when the pictures were taken. The timestamp suggested it was the evening that Elise had been killed, but Finley couldn't remember taking them. It was only when she saw the wide-angle view of the back of the hotel that she remembered walking out onto the green to take some parting shots before she caught her runaway flight back to Delhi. *I was so close. So close to gone. Now, I'm so glad I stayed. God looks after children and fools. So glad She is looking after me!*

She slowly advanced the sequence. She remembered putting the setting on automatic so that she could capture the panorama. She had panned the camera across the grounds, starting at one corner of the building and ending on the other side.

In the frames, she could see Elise get up from her café table near one of the pillars on the terrace and head to where the palmist was seated. She and Sandra had been so excited about having a resident palm reader. Presumably, in this shot, she is making an appointment. Not long after, a waiter comes to her vacated table and puts a thermos in her bag. An identical water bottle is then seen on his tray as he walks away.

"What the he . . .?" Finley only realized she had said the words out loud when Max, freshly scrubbed and still dripping water, came over in concern.

CARTER FIELDING

"What's the matter? Are you in pain?" He dropped to his knees to get a better look at her face. "Is it your head? Shall I get a doctor?"

Finley turned and stared, only then realizing his misunderstanding. "No, no. I'm fine. I just found what Evans and Das were looking for. Can you pass me my phone, please?"

While she talked to Evans and explained the photos she had, she scrolled through the sequence for Max. When he saw the scenario playing out on the screen, his reaction was the same as hers. "Holy sh . . . !"

Evans and Das were at their door in fifteen minutes. By then, Max was dried and dressed. Finley repeated the sequence for the two inspectors and sat watching their faces.

"Bloody hell! We've got him. Whoever he is, he's ours." Evans got up and planted a kiss on Finley's cheek, a grin invading his face as he spoke, "You are brilliant! Absolutely brilliant."

Finley held out another thumb drive to Das. "I have no choice but to leave Jaipur now. This is my last thumb drive!"

"I will return them all before you leave, I promise," Das assured her. "Thank you again for your help."

Max showed both men to the door. Das had already started down the hall, but Evans held back to catch Max's eye. "I see you saw the light, as they say."

"I did," Max replied with a half laugh. "I may still be a fool, but I'm her fool."

Evans simply nodded and followed Das to the lobby.

The next morning, Max and Finley slept in. They worried, when they did finally rouse themselves out of bed, that they had missed breakfast. When they arrived on the terrace, they grabbed their usual table. David and Whitt were nowhere around.

"They must have come to breakfast early." Finley pulled apart her ginger paratha and spooned on a dab of sweet chutney.

"So, you beat us to breakfast, eh?" Whitt slipped into a seat beside Finley, deftly extracted the paratha from her fingers, and popped it in her mouth before Finley could protest.

"You have to get me another one!" Finley wiped chutney from her sister's cheek. "Goodness, you're a messy eater."

Whitt flashed her sister a smile and headed toward the buffet with David in tow. When she returned some minutes later, Evans had joined their table. Still pretending he was Meadows, he turned on the gregarious charm as he ordered his coffee and perused the morning offerings that graced the group's plates.

"I think it is English breakfast for me today," he concluded, "but I need a lot of coffee first."

"Burning the candle at both ends again?" Whitt asked, as she plopped down in her seat and deposited a fresh ginger paratha on her sister's plate.

"Your sister kept me busy last night." Evans smiled at the suggestive nature of the comment, as he went on to explain, "She found an interesting piece of evidence."

"What? Something else happened after you went to the room?" David was incredulous.

"Finley found an answer to who one of the moles might be and how the poison had gotten into Elise's water thermos," Max related, accepting Finley's offer of the other half of her paratha.

"Who is it and how did they do it?" Whitt asked excitedly. She turned to her sister with a pout. "And you didn't tell me first!"

"It was late. I figured you guys were asleep," Finley said.

"You two can make up later. Who was it?" David asked.

Evans smiled at the exchange. He could see that the play fights that had begun some twenty-plus years before would continue into eternity, as long as there was breath in the sisters' lungs. He envied that kind of closeness. But before he could respond, he felt a light tap on his shoulder.

"Mr. Meadows." It was Sandra, again adorned in jewels. She had clearly recovered her cache of jewelry. "I wanted to say goodbye. I'm heading off to Kashmir to an ayurvedic spa. The hotel recommended it to me. It was their gift, after all that had happened."

Whitt whispered under her breath, "Better a free boondoggle that a highly visible suit."

Sandra continued, directing her comments solely to Evans/Meadows. "I wanted to thank you for all of your help. You have been a most gracious travel companion. I do hope we have occasion to meet again."

Evans assumed his Meadows persona and stood to take Sandra's hand. "The pleasure was all mine, my dear lady."

"I have a question to ask you. It may seem a bit indiscreet, though," Sandra murmured, her voice barely above a whisper. She paused and drew a breath. "After I was attacked, did you come to my room?"

Evans smiled gallantly. "I wish I had come earlier to protect you. Both Logan and I were of the same sentiment when we heard of your unfortunate circumstances. But, no, I was never in your room. Finley found you."

"That was what the staff said when I asked. It must have been the medicine the doctor gave me." She chuckled. "You must think I'm mad. I promise I won't stalk you."

"I would be honored if you did." Evans gave her a sly smile and gently kissed her hand. "Travel safely and enjoy your restorative."

When Sandra had said her goodbyes and headed off toward the lobby, Evans sighed. He looked at Finley with a crooked smile, shaking his head.

"That's the part of this job I hate most. Lying to innocent people. In order to keep them innocent."

"You did the right thing," Finley confirmed. "It would have been too complicated."

Both Evans and Finley turned to a wall of confused faces.

"So, what was all that about?" Whitt whined. "Something else you failed to tell me?"

Evans laughed. All the envy of their sibling closeness melted away. He would have strangled a younger sister or brother under the barrage of constant needling and rivalry. He began to explain to those at the table Sandra's confusion and the circumstances around it.

"In order to get into the room after Sandra's attack without blowing my cover, I had to play her ardent suitor. Finley was witness to it. I must have been sufficiently convincing. Poor Sandra remembered it, even under a sedative-induced stupor."

"You had me fooled," Finley snickered, replaying the scene of Evans down on one knee, fawning over the befuddled Sandra.

"Can we get back to the murder now?" David was getting exasperated. "Who did it? You stopped right at the good part."

"Sorry for the interruption. It was a repeat criminal named John Austin, aka Arun Kumar. He worked for another trafficking element, but it appears that the two syndicates may have joined forces. Or Kumar is just playing both ends against the middle."

"Did you arrest him already?" Max asked. "Or are we vulnerable?"

"No, you are all safe." Evans's eyes rested on Finley. "We picked him up early this morning. Hence my bleary-eyed state. I will be functioning today on less than two hours sleep."

"There are a couple of other questions that haven't been answered for me," Finley queried. "First, where did the necklace go? And second, why did Devya lie?"

"And if I answer those, and confirm that Das had your thumb drives delivered to your room, will you two consider the case closed?" Evans asked, looking for an answer from Whitt and Finley. They both nodded.

"The necklace slipped into the water when Elise fell into the reflecting pool. One of the officers found it early in the investigation and entered into evidence," Evans replied. "I can see why Banerjee and his syndicate wanted it so badly. That ruby had a market value of over $100,000."

David and Max both whistled when Evans gave the amount. David recovered first. "Damn, that was a pretty substantial stone."

Evans smiled. "As to the other question, Devya lied about the happy-home scene over dinner because she and Ravi had indeed argued, and she didn't want to be implicated if something happened to him."

"So, she preferred to lie and throw the police off rather than give full disclosure and find her missing husband." Whitt shook her head. "That's cold."

The group sat quietly for a few minutes, taking in all that had happened. Max broke the silence. "Will you be staying on in India much longer?"

"Another week or so to be sure that we have this case fully closed out and then back to Lyon." Evans wondered whether Max's curiosity was purely idle or was motivated by his desire to be sure that Evans was as far away from Finley as possible. He hoped the events of the last couple of days had taught Max a lesson about trust, especially about trusting a woman as dear as Finley.

The rest of the morning and early afternoon was spent packing and making the rounds to say goodbye. The couple from the UAE that they had not had much opportunity to speak to had stopped by their table as they were finishing breakfast to say their farewells. Finley had seen Hema's parents in the arcade when she had gone into the shop looking for another pair of headphones. They had asked scarcely veiled questions about Logan and his reputation. It was clear that they wanted to know whether they could entrust their daughter to a man like Logan.

"I have known Logan for three years, if not more, by now. He is one of the sweetest, dearest, most generous people I know. And smart, to boot," Finley had said.

"Then, why did you not marry him?" Hema's father asked with a gleam in his eye.

"Because my heart belongs to someone else," Finley replied with a smile.

As she walked back to her room, she hoped that Logan had indeed found someone in Hema to whom he could give his heart, knowing it was safe and treasured. She knew they were only getting to know each other and had many a trial to pass in their relationship, but her gut told her that Hema was something good. And Logan deserved good.

Hema and Logan were waiting in the lobby when the Four Musketeers came down later in the day to check out. Much to Max's consternation, the bill for the rooms, meals, and all services had been paid. Finley sidled over and took his hand.

"Be gracious. It's just Logan's way," she whispered. "You can send him an extra special thank-you gift later."

Max squeezed her hand in agreement as they rejoined the group.

"I am so glad that I met you." Hema leaned over and kissed Finley on the cheek. As she straightened up, she exchanged a shy glance with Logan. "And him."

"Well. I can't tell you how glad I am that the two of you found each other. He's a good man."

Hema nodded in agreement as she went to stand at Logan's side.

Max and Logan had taken the time when the women were conversing to say their goodbyes.

"Sorry I gave you such a hard time. It was difficult for me to understand the nature and extent of your friendship with Finley. I hope we can have a more civil relationship next time we meet," Max offered, as the two stood together watching Finley and Hema talking.

"No problem. I can understand your thinking. If another man looked at Hema, I think I would jump to the same conclusions—and I'm just getting to know her. Nothing nearly as complex as your relationship with Finley," Logan mused.

He turned to face Max. "But I want you to know that you could never be loved more deeply by any woman than you are by that one. I envy you. Just hope I get there one day."

"I know. Now. And it is returned a hundredfold." Max smiled and shook Logan's hand.

On the plane, the two couples took advantage of the cabin space, each claiming a table and seats across the aisle from each other. Within minutes of sitting down, both David and Whitt were dead asleep, curled up in each other's arms. The flight attendant placed their glasses of champagne in the cupholders and retreated.

"I wonder what they did all night that has them so tuckered out," Finley said wryly.

"Probably the same thing we did." Max took the playful punch he received in reply in good grace.

He continued, "Look, as fate, or luck, would have it, the data from this healthcare project is coming in with sufficient consistency that the government is moving forward with the recommended changes to the healthcare policy."

"What does that mean for you?" Finley asked tentatively, her head rising from his shoulder to catch a glimpse of what his face was telling her.

"It means that I can wrap this project up in the next couple of weeks, and then I'm free to go wherever you go for the next year or so." Max proposed, "How does that sound to you?"

"Really? We can go anywhere?" Finley asked. Max had brought up the idea of him taking time off to travel with Finley several months ago when they were in Colombo. But Finley hadn't really thought it was possible. Yet now, it was going to happen.

"Anywhere. Just call Dan up and tell him to give you the most fun, meaty assignment he has," Max proffered. "Or, better yet, design your own. Where would you go if money were no object?"

"Now you are starting to sound like Logan."

"He asked you that?" Max gave her a side-glance.

Finley nodded. "Yep. Several times when I returned to New York the first time. And all I could think of was coming back to you."

"Oh, Fin." He took her face in his hands and stared at her, before kissing her gently. "How can you love such a stupid man?"

"I don't think I have much choice in the matter. My ticker has a mind of its own. And it chose you."

"But you really were going to leave for good this time, weren't you?" He was still looking at her intently.

She closed her eyes and breathed in deeply. She slowly opened her eyes and held his gaze. "Yes. I was packed and had booked a flight back to Delhi. Survival dictated that I had to leave. I think Elise, in a strange way, was our guardian angel."

"I am so glad you didn't leave." Max kissed her forehead, her nose, and her lips, before pulling her close and holding her.

"Me, too."

Finley's phone started ringing almost the minute the plane touched down. Whitt mouthed that Mama had called her, too.

"Mama, what's wrong? Are you and Daddy okay?" Finley breathed anxiously into the phone, as she got into the back of the car that was to take them to Max's apartment.

"Yes, dear, we are both quite fine. Sorry to worry you," Mama responded. "We just want to let you know that Daddy has given me a trip to London as my anniversary present. I want you and your sister—and your partners—to come join us for the celebration in two weeks."

She paused before finishing her thought. "I am trying to be progressive! So be sure that David and Max come. Daddy said to let you all know that he is footing the bill for this little extravaganza so there should be no reason that you can't come."

That final phrase had turned an invitation into an edict. Mama expected them all to be there, and with bells on.

"Yes, ma'am. Whitt's here with me, so I will let her know."

"Well, I won't keep you. I'll send you the details so you can make flight arrangements. I can't wait to see you. And meet those handsome men that have you both so enraptured." She signed off. "Your daddy sends his love. Bye, darlings."

She was gone before Finley could even finish saying, "I love you."

Whitt had leaned forward so she was eye to eye with her sister. "Are they all right?"

"Yeah. She just wanted to invite us all to London for their anniversary bash. That's what Daddy gave her as a gift. And that includes significant others." Finley sat back and thought about what she would have told Mama only two days ago had she and Max split up. She didn't want to even think about it.

Max laid his head on her shoulder and buried his nose in her hair. What was he to her now? Whitt and David were engaged, but what were he and Finley? Boyfriend and girlfriend? That sounded a bit too juvenile. Partners? That felt ambiguous. Significant others worked but still didn't have the significance he was looking for. He would think on it.

He whispered, "You mentioned that the invitation included significant others. Does that include me?"

She turned her head to engage him. Her gaze was tender but unnervingly direct. His heart fluttered at her words. "You tell me."

The End

If you enjoyed this book and want to learn
more about Finley and Whitt Blake
join our mailing list at www.mcarterfielding.com or
drop me a line at carter.fielding6554@gmail.com.
I'd love to hear from you.
Talk soon!

**Read on to get a sneak peek at the next book in
the Blake Sisters Travel Mystery series.**

ACKNOWLEDGEMENTS

As I have told readers before, often when I sit down to write, I don't know where the book is going or how it will end. In this case, I had a fairly good idea of both. That was mainly because you, the readers, gave me an idea of what you wanted, needed to hear from the characters. So, thanks—

- to my always supportive cousins, who help me sift through reader suggestions and plot the Four Musketeers' trek across the world;
- to my parents, who are rather enjoying these stories in a genre that they had never heard of before;
- to my beta and advance reading team, who keep me honest in my depiction of the time and place, and most importantly, the characters;
- to my friends, who have been enthusiastic in their praise and gentle in their suggestions;
- to the Bublish production and distribution team, who have held my hand from day one and keep teaching me things about editing, formatting, and promotion that ensure that getting a good story into the hands of readers is always our first priority; and

- to the growing flock of "Fieldlings," who keep surprising me with your engagement with the characters—and with me online.

We have only just begun!

AUTHOR BIO

Carter Fielding is a millennial with an old soul. She likes old maps, old photographs, vintage records, and vintage champagnes. A Southerner with roots in Anderson, South Carolina, she likes a good bourbon, a day that calls for wearing a barn jacket and a pair of wellies, and the smell of wet earth after a good rain. She started writing the Blake Sisters series during lockdown to tame a wanderlust that couldn't be satisfied by a trip to Harris Teeter and ended up building a relationship with the whole cast of characters that has taken on a life of its own. She lives in Northern Virginia with her Boykin Spaniel, Trucker, and uses her passion for books and travel to create characters she hopes readers will love.

A Blake Sisters Travel Mystery
Book 4
Murder in the Marshes

Carter Fielding

CHAPTER 1

HOME. THE NOTION OF "HOME" had never struck her like it did when Max said it. Maybe it was the newness of him back in her life. Maybe it was the fear that what he called "home" might be different from what she had in mind. Whatever it was, Finley Blake paused when Max asked if she was excited to be heading home.

"What is the first thing you'll do when you get home?" asked Max Davies, her partner in life for the last ten months and for the next hundred years, as they talked about the plans for her sister's wedding in Charleston that was only four weeks away.

They were sitting in their mews house in Chelsea on a raw April morning. It had taken Finley a little while to get used to calling it "their" house. In her mind, it had always been "Max's" house. He had owned it when they'd been together seven years ago in Tangier and when they'd split some two years later. He had still owned it when they'd reconnected in Tangier, almost two years ago to the day.

It hadn't become "theirs" until several months ago, when he had stood in the study just down the hall from where they now sat, during Whitt's engagement party, and slipped the spectacular diamond, yellow and white gold band on her finger. He had pledged his everlasting love and asked her to join him on an endless journey through life. It hadn't been a marriage, but rather a life commitment. Max had a thing about marriage. When he had explained his aversion to the institution, Finley had understood. She wasn't in love with marriage. She was desperately, and forever, in love with him. So, they had settled into blissful cohabitation in "committed permanence without marriage."

Max brought her mental wanderings back to the present. "When I was traveling and would finally get back here—home— my first thing was a whiskey in the back garden. I'd drop my bag at the stairs, grab my mail, select a single malt, and head to the garden—even in the rain. The mist was never heavy with the cover of the trees."

His voice trailed off, and Finley looked at him, deep in his reminiscence of that first taste of home. Finley had to think about what she did first when she walked through the door, back from a trip. To a degree, it depended on where she had landed at the end of the voyage. When she was in New York, before she and Max had firmly taken root together and she had transplanted herself in London, she would order Thai or Lebanese from her favorite take-out place on Amsterdam, even before her shoes were off. Then she would pour herself a glass of wine and flip through the mound of mail that had accumulated in the weeks she'd been gone.

If she was in Chevy Chase, camping at Mama and Daddy's on the return leg, she would get deposited at the kitchen island on a stool, with an elegant flute of champagne or prosecco in front of her, while Daddy took her bag upstairs to her room and Mama finished putting dinner together. Since she had been in London with Max, she had followed his patterns, not yet establishing a "welcome home" rhythm that was uniquely her own.

"I don't know. I guess it depends," Finley finally responded. Max stood to refill her mug with the Ugandan blend she'd brought back from a reconnaissance trip to East and Central Africa a few weeks before. "Coffee or wine figures significantly into the equation wherever home is at the time and whenever I get there."

"But isn't there something that you miss? That you think about the longer you're away, as you get more homesick? That shows up in your dreams, that you can taste on your tongue?" Max got more animated as he threw out each question, as if to provoke her mind into remembering something. Anything.

Finley watched him warm to the subject. His eyes widened as he spoke, and his lips met, as if tasting something memorable, something evocative of the tastes and smells that assured him he was finally home. She smiled, enjoying his excitement. Yet, she still shook her head. "Nope. Nothing comes to mind. Nothing that happens every time I get back from a trip. Heck, most of the time, I don't even know where home is. Sometimes New York, sometimes with you in Delhi or here in London, sometimes in DC, sometimes in Charleston. I'll have to think about it."

"Interesting," was all Max said, as he scanned her face. After a minute, he leaned down and brushed his lips on hers before returning to kiss her fully. "Home is where the heart is, so they say. Where is your heart, darling?"

"Wherever you are," she murmured quietly, tilting her head to look up at him and catching the chiseled angle of his jaw in the filtered light. "And therein lies the trouble. Since you—we—are everywhere." She took his face in her hands and traveled its plains and valleys with her eyes. She traced her thumbs along the laugh lines that framed his mouth before embracing his lips with hers.

When they parted, Max studied her eyes in return. Eventually he spoke. "So, what's the plan for next month? I know your mother has an agenda that we are to follow. I also know that you have work to do before we head to Charleston, so fill me in."

"The most important thing for me right now is prepping for this trip to Tanzania. I'm so glad they brought me back in to do the follow-up on the story we did last year."

Finley reached over and tore off the end of the almond croissant Max had just put on his plate. She put one crusty horn on the edge of her napkin and then leaned over to tear off the other end. Max sipped his coffee as he watched her work. They had long ago agreed to this division of eating labor, since Max liked the soft innards of most foods and Finley liked the crispy outsides. It worked for most things they ate. They had yet to come across anything where they both reached for the same portion. She popped a sliced almond into her mouth. "The backstory on the shift in the great migration cycles because of climate change is a nice angle for the piece that *Traveler's Tales* is doing. And a documentary, too. A nice departure."

"Where are you going to be?" Max munched on his piece of the croissant. "And when do you leave again?"

"I leave at the end of next week and will only be gone for a couple of weeks," Finley relayed. "I'll be flying into Arusha but then taking a prop into Serengeti National Park. I may head over to the crater," she said, referring to the Ngorongoro Crater, an ancient caldera that was home to leopards, black rhinos, and lions.

She continued, "I'll come back here, though, before we go. We'll have a few days before we head to South Carolina. I'll need to repack. My mother would not appreciate me showing up for a wedding—a Southern wedding no less—with only boots and khakis in my bag!"

Max chortled at the imaginary look of disgust and dismay on Mama's face if field gear had been Finley's only attire. "Are all the women in your family as persnickety as your mother?"

"Well, I'm not, and Whitt isn't."

"You, no. But Whitt can be a little high-maintenance, you have to admit," Max reminded her gently. He waited for her reaction.

Finley grinned. "Yes. The girl can be a handful at times." She thought for a moment. "Quite honestly, the Blake *and* Montgomery women—and you'll get to meet both sides—run the gamut. Some are easygoing, others are prickly. And others can be downright rude in that subtle, Southern way. Most all of us are obstinate and opinionated, even the ones that look like shrinking violets. Don't let that facade fool you. The term 'steel magnolias' was created for a reason—to describe Southern women."

Max slipped behind her and draped his arms around her shoulders. "Is my darling girl admitting to being a little bullheaded at times?"

"Only when necessary." She turned and planted a kiss on his chin. "Only when wholly necessary."

Max returned to his side of the island and began clearing away the dishes. "So, what do you have planned for the rest of the day? I have some project RFPs I need to review. My year of following after you will be over before we know it, and I need to have some consulting work to go back to."

"I need to look at the Serengeti contact sheets from last year to see which of those photos I can use, and then I need to scope out the storyline I want to try. That should take me until next week!" Finley rose and moved her mug to the dishwasher. "Or at least until dinner."

Max chuckled. "It won't be that bad if you focus."

"That's a big if."

"So we don't have to worry about dinner, let's go out. And I'll find a place, so you don't even have to think of that."

Finley went to Max and wrapped her arms around him. "You are just too good to me!" She released him with a peck on his cheek before heading upstairs to her study.

When she had moved in, Max had wanted to give up a portion of his downstairs study for her so they could work in proximity to each other. After a few days, in which his conference calls had disrupted her concentration while writing, she had quietly moved her things to the smaller of the spare bedrooms upstairs. He hadn't said anything. Rather, he made periodic trips up the stairs to check on her, often saying nothing during his passage down the hall, but always sticking his head in to glance at her as she worked.

Finley opened her computer and started scrolling through the contact sheets. Page upon page of the animals, people, and scenery that the earlier camera crew had shot almost seven months earlier came to life on the screen. She hadn't been in Tanzania to see the migration, having been called in at the last minute as backup to cover the Zanzibar leg after the principal team had been pulled to film a tiger trek in India. She and Max had used it as a mini-honeymoon, since the Zanzibar trip had come shortly after they'd committed to each other.

Finley took the opportunity now to carefully examine each frame on the sheet and take in the powerful stories that had been frozen in time. Sam, the principal photographer for the shoot, had marked the frames that she liked best, providing a caption for most of them in addition to the date and location. As Finley located a preferred shot among the numerous photos on a page, she would glance at the ten or so shots before and after to see whether she agreed with Sam's assessment. Sam's eye was so attuned to light and color that there were often as many as three or four great shots to choose from. In that instance, Finley went for either the one that had the greatest action or the one that told the most compelling story.

Even though the timing of her trip would be too early to catch the wildebeest crossing of the Mara River that most associate with the great migration, Finley was looking forward to spending the latter part of the calving season in Serengeti National Park with the park staff—the rangers, vets, trackers, and guides who balanced the preferences of the tourists, who were the financial fuel of the park, with the needs of the animals and terrain that were its lifeblood.

Traveler's Tales had decided that the time was right for a conversation around climate change and its impact on tourism. Dan Burton, her editor at the magazine and a former law school classmate, had selected Finley to capture the story at both Serengeti and Maasai Mara. Other teams were being dispatched to Kodiak National Wildlife Refuge in Alaska, Yala National Park in Sri Lanka, the Great Barrier Reef in Australia, and several other locations around the world to film portions of a documentary the magazine was compiling. It was new territory for the magazine, a departure from its print format, but no less hard-hitting than some of its other stories on identity theft and human trafficking. Finley had contributed significantly to the latter story.

Her concentration was broken by the ringing of her cellphone and the picture of her sister Whitt's face popping up on her screen.

"Hey, kid. What's up?" Finley asked. "Where are you?"

"Mumbai still. The project is delayed a few weeks, but I should be able to make it to Charleston without too much hassle. David is flying into Doha from Tbilisi, and we'll meet there. We'll see you at home at the end of the month."

"You sound pretty casual about making it home for the wedding. You sure the delays won't trip you up? You and David are pretty important players." Finley surveyed her sister's face on the screen. She seemed calm and normal, but with Whitt, it was hard to tell. The hotel could be on fire and Whitt would continue the conversation as if nothing were amiss. "Everything all right? You guys aren't getting cold feet, are you?"

"No, we're okay. David is a little nervous about meeting the whole clan, but I told him if it gets too much, we'll just grab you and Max and head off to the justice of the peace." Whitt paused for effect. "Or Vegas! We never wanted a big wedding anyway."

"Mama would kill you! She's been working her tuchus off for this wedding. And whether you want it or not, she's going to have it, even if she has to kidnap you two to get you there!" Finley laughed at the thought of Whitt and David being carried down the aisle with gunnysacks over their heads and dropped at the altar. *Don't mess with Mama, girl. It'll get ugly, and there is no way you're going to win!*

"I know. But I refuse to stress over this project or my wedding. So, the Reserve Bank of India's delays are not going to ruffle me. Nor is David's request to add more fraternity brothers to the guest list. Even Mama questioning my decision not to wear a veil isn't going to get a reaction."

"That's the attitude. This is your wedding, and you call the shots." Finley knew how it would go down. Whitt would state her preferences. Mama would purse her lips before giving a radiant smile, nodding her head in agreement—and then she would go off and do whatever she darn well pleased.

"When do you and Max get in? And thank you so much for suggesting and arranging the Airbnb in town, instead of us staying on Sullivan's Island." Whitt sighed. "I love what Mama and all are doing for us, but that house is going to be crazy and all the questions and suggestions and such would just send me around the bend. If I'm not there already."

"It will give us a little time together, too. Max and I will run interference with Mama, so don't worry. She's just excited. This is the only chance she's going to get to do this wedding thing."

"You and Max still aren't ever going to jump the broom?"

"Nope. We're happy with the way things are. I understand how the trauma from his parents' divorce soured him on marriage. But it didn't sour him on commitment. We're no less married than if we had gone to the courthouse."

"I know and Mama and Daddy understand, but be prepared for whispering at the house." Whitt shook her head. "Tongues'll be wagging."

"And I'll just redirect them back your way. This is your day, and nothing is going to mar that!" Finley beamed at her sister. "In only a month, you and David will be married! Who'd have thunk it, kid!"

"Not me. I figured I'd be the last one to walk down the aisle and that you surely would've. You can never tell!"

"Speaking of not telling . . . Mama still hasn't figured out that you switched the guest list she sent to the calligrapher?" Finley stared at Whitt through the screen, her eyes wide. "How the heck did you pull that off? More importantly, what are you going to say when she discovers it?"

"'Sorry, I must have pulled the wrong file?'" Whitt snickered under her breath before letting loose her indignation. "She had fifth cousins twice removed on there who we haven't seen in a month of Sundays! It's bad enough I have to put up with having Cousin Tommy and Lael there, plus all of the cousins on Daddy's side. I told her I wanted a small wedding, and that is something I won't surrender on."

"Well, you may win on this one. It would be inappropriate to send out invitations this late. Mama will just have to suck it up."

Whitt chuckled again. "Yep, that she will. Look, before I forget what I called you for . . . it's about Evans. Is there space in the house for him to stay a couple of nights? He will be coming in the night of the rehearsal dinner and leaving on Sunday, so it literally is just a couple of nights. I'd like to accommodate him if we can."

Chief Inspector Gareth Evans, an Interpol agent who had recently been promoted, had on more than one occasion saved the sisters' necks. That said, they had returned the favor in Sri Lanka, rescuing him from certain death. After all they had been through together, it seemed wrong not to invite him to the wedding.

"The house has seven bedrooms and a study, so even with Charlie, Kirsten and Reid, Logan and Hema, and Mooney and her new beau, there is more than enough room." Finley enumerated. "And then we rented the other house on Montagu, too, and that one has five rooms and a sleeping porch. I don't think it's booked up with the Blake cousins yet. There is more than enough space."

"What about Max?"

"What about him? He'll be fine with it," Finley smirked. "And, if he's not, he can sleep on the couch! It was crazy in the first place that he ever thought there was anything between Evans and me. If he is still jealous after all this time, he needs to check himself."

"Easier said than done with Max. That man guards you like Fort Knox. I'm just trying to head off potential issues before they happen. I'd hate for guests to come to blows at my wedding."

Finley snorted with laughter. "That would never happen with those two. Evans is too buttoned-up British, and Max would never allow himself to lose control like that. Nah, they might glare at each other, but they'd never duke it out. And over what? That storm passed long ago."

"I hope so. Then it's settled. Evans is in the Rutledge house with all of us. I'd better get going. Got a list a mile long of things I need to take care of. Thanks loads. Love you. And love to Max."

"Back at you. Love to David. See you in a few weeks!"

When Finley put the phone down, Max was standing at the door, smiling. "I knew it sounded like too much fun up here for you to be working! How's Whitt doing? Got a case of nerves?"

"No, she's really calm, which I should've expected. She may toss her cookies before she walks down the aisle, but nary a guest will ever know." Finley decided to lob the Evans grenade and see how it landed. "She wanted to know if there was room in our house for Evans to stay a few nights. I told her I thought we could fit him in."

Max stood next to her, his eyes on the shot she had just pulled up of a lion bringing down a wildebeest. He tapped the screen. "Nice shot! On Evans, sure. If there's room. Goodness knows you two owe the man your lives. And on more than one occasion!"

"Thanks, babe! That's one thing off my chest." Finley exhaled.

"What? You thought I would object? Why?"

"Well, the two of you have never exactly been BFFs!"

"Acknowledged, but hey, I won the girl, so no hard feelings." He claimed his prize with a thorough kiss that left her a little light-headed. "You ready for dinner? We have reservations in an hour, but if now isn't a good time for you to stop, I can move them."

"Nope, this is perfect timing. I just finished creating my final card. I'll take a few clean memory cards just in case I want a different mix, but this will get me started." Finley turned off the computer and closed it. "Where are we heading?"

"A surprise!"

The surprise turned out to be Le Colombier, one of her favorite restaurants, a modern bistro on the edge of their neighborhood. For reasons she couldn't remember, they hadn't visited it since they'd returned from Delhi. Max beamed as she recognized the direction they were walking and squeezed his hand in anticipation.

"Thank you! I had almost forgotten about this little place."

"I'm glad you still like it." Max kissed her forehead as they neared the entrance. "Maybe this can be *our* 'welcome home' routine. We'll drop the bags and head here, to a table in the back corner, and decompress. I'll have my single malt here with you, in the back garden if it's warm or at the back table if it's too cold."

"Done. What a lovely new tradition!" Finley grinned as she settled into her seat. They were seated at a table inside since the April evening had turned chilly. She'd thrown on a black, midi-length ribbed-knit dress, with a blush blazer and strappy, black kitten heels, not knowing exactly how upscale they were going. Max hadn't given her any clues when he'd pulled on a pair of charcoal trousers, his signature marine-blue shirt, and a blue-and-green houndstooth jacket. He wasn't in jeans, but with what he had on, he could have been going to an afternoon gallery opening, with the addition of a tie and pocket square, or down the street to his favorite wine shop to place another order. *Men's clothing is so ambiguous! At times like this, I need Mooney to help style me,* Finley had thought as she'd gotten dressed.

Sitting there now, though, it didn't matter. Max, looking at her like she hung the moon, made her feel regal, whether she had on a tiara or cutoffs. She marveled at how close they had come to walking away from each other forever. How this creating of their special traditions might never have happened.

"What are you thinking?" Max reached across the table and took her hand in his. "You look awfully pensive. That scares me!"

"Does it? Why? What do you think I'm going to say? If I'm unhappy or puzzled, I've learned to put the issue on the table rather than pocket it." *A realization that might have saved a lot of heartache if it had come earlier, eh, girlfriend?* "And right now, I'm deliriously happy!"

"Are you?" Max sat back in his chair and watched her face break into a grin that had the corners of her eyes dancing. "What are you so happy about?"

"Everything! Being here with you, heading to Tanzania, Whitt and David getting married, seeing my family."

"Tell me about this family of yours. I've met your parents and heard a bit about your cousin, Odessa, but tell me about some of the others."

Finley took a slow sip of her Riesling. It was dry and surprisingly full-bodied, with the aromatic fruitiness she liked. If she had wine at any of her family's houses, except Mama and Daddy's, it was likely to be sweet like the iced tea. She would have to warn Max to stick to beer or bourbon.

What could she tell him about her family that wouldn't overwhelm him or scare him off? There would be a lot of them, that was for sure, since both sides would be coming, and that meant extended as well as immediate family. She thought back on all the times the Sullivan's Island house had been overrun with family, usually for weddings or funerals. Those were the times everyone felt compelled to make a showing. While the adults talked or cooked, or talked while they cooked, the kids, all cousins by blood or friendship, would play tag or red-light-green-light in the expansive backyard, which would soon be decorated for Whitt's wedding.

Her mind wandered back to one of those summers. Finley had been about twelve or thirteen, and Whitt six or so. They had slipped away from the rest of the pack and headed up the stairs that led to the widow's walk circling the uppermost level of the house. They had wanted to see the water that was visible from both the front and the back of that level—the ocean on the front side and the marshes on the back. They had only been on the deck for a few minutes when they heard snickering and saw the hatch door drop. Before they could reach it, the door slammed shut. They heard the bolt engage and knew they were locked out. The noise of all the people on the porch and in the yard muffled their cries for help, and after a few minutes, they sat and watched as the sun slipped below the horizon and night started to creep in. When Daddy found them some time later, Finley had used the skirt of her dress to cover her sister and was singing her to sleep.

Daddy was merciless in his punishment of the perpetrators. He never said a word, but when dessert—a humungous chocolate layer cake and homemade vanilla bean ice cream—was passed around that evening, Daddy made sure that the miscreants were skipped. His glare dared them to protest. Finley never did forgive Lael and Tommy for that prank. She wasn't sure she ever would.